BOLD COAST *Love*

BY
Diana Tremain Braund

Bella
BOOKS

Ferndale, Michigan
2000

Bella Books, Inc.
P.O. Box 201007
Ferndale, MI 48220

Printed in the United States of America on acid-free paper
First Edition

Editor: Lila Empson
Cover designer: Bonnie Liss (Phoenix Graphics)

ISBN 0-9677753-2-9

To my sister, Annie.
The one constant in my life.

About the Author

The author continues to live and work in rural Maine, where this book is set. She enjoys reading and writing and is now working on a book of poetry. She takes long walks on the beach with her all-American female dog, Bob. Braund also has written two other books set in Maine, *The Way Life Should Be* and *Wicked Good Time*, both published by Naiad Press.

Visit
Bella Books
at

www.bellabooks.com

Chapter 1

Jackie frowned at the reception room clock. Three o'clock, and still no Dana. She noticed that Vera was watching her. "I guess I'm anxious," she said quietly.

Carin, her arms full of files, looked up from where she was standing. "Are you waiting for someone?" She smiled at Jackie.

"Just a friend. She should have been here hours ago. But on-time airline arrivals are one of America's greatest oxymorons." Jackie looked at the door again, willing it to open.

"I agree. Why the last time Darrel and I flew — we were going to see my folks in Atlanta — we were stranded for hours in the airport. Some kind of engine problem. I thought that man of mine was going to tear some heads off. I kept telling him to calm down, but he just fumed. When we finally got out of there, I bought him a drink on the plane, just to calm his nerves." Vera smiled at Jackie and then added quietly, "Don't go tearing anyone's heads off, okay?"

"Not likely." Jackie studied the file Vera had handed her, but her mind refused to focus on the lab report. All she could think about was Dana and the endless airports they had shared. Their jobs often kept them on opposite continents. She and Dana had been together for three years, although added together in real time, it was only two years. Jackie hated the separation. During the long months apart, their only link was an international telephone that often crackled and hissed. Dana intensified her life the weeks they were together, yet Jackie's energy ebbed with each departure, fatigue settling comfortably around her like a woolen shawl. They had talked on the telephone the night before — Dana from her hotel in Europe where she'd been on a photo assignment, Jackie from their home on the bold coast of Maine — and tried to coordinate their schedules. If everything had gone according to plan, Dana would have been at the clinic by nine A.M.

Vera smiled. "She'll get here."

Jackie willed herself to concentrate on the file. She looked up only when she heard the clinic door open.

"Hi."

The frown on Jackie's face dissolved into a smile. "Hi, yourself," Jackie said quietly. A tsunami of emotions washed over her as she looked at her lover.

Vera watched Carin's expression change as she took in the beauty of the woman standing at the door. She read Carin's reaction as her eyes took in Dana's designer jeans and white shirt, casual yet exotic. Dana would make a tattered flour sack look fashionable, Vera thought. "Oh, sweetie," Vera jumped up and dashed around the receptionist's desk even before Jackie had a chance to move. She hugged Dana.

"I've missed you," Dana said, looking at Jackie across Vera's shoulder.

"You've been missed," Vera held Dana at arm's length and then pulled her against her. "When did you get in?"

Dana hugged her tightly and stepped back.

"A short time ago, I came directly from the airport."

Dana untangled herself from Vera's arms and gave Jackie a sisterly hug. "I'd love to talk to you in your office." Dana pushed her fiery-red hair off her forehead.

Carin noisily set the files she had been holding on Vera's desk. She looked from Vera to Jackie.

"Oh, I'm forgetting my manners. Dana Bradley, my nurse Carin Chase," Jackie said.

"How do you do." Dana extended her hand.

Carin took Dana's hand, "Pleased to meet you. Are you visiting the area?"

Dana smiled, "Something like that."

"I was just telling Vera and the doctor how my husband just hates flying. The last time I was able to get him on an airplane, I thought he was going to pop an artery —"

"Carin," Vera interrupted. "We have patients waiting. Why don't you see to it that Mrs. Clark gets set up in room one? Miss Danforth will be here in a few minutes, and let's put her in room two."

"Of course." Vera could see the disappointment on Carin's face.

Carin took the files Vera had handed her. "Nice to meet you. Hope we get a chance to visit while you're here." Carin smiled at Dana.

"That would be nice." Dana said quietly.

"Go," Vera ordered before Jackie could say anything. "I'll

3

have Carin get everyone set up; that will give you a few minutes." She said it so only they could hear.

Dana kissed her aunt on the cheek. "Thanks."

Dana hooked her arm through Jackie's and walked toward the doctor's office. "I have planned a more visual way of expressing myself once we are alone," she whispered under her breath.

Jackie felt her passion awakening. She marveled at Dana's unflagging resiliency. She had been on an airplane for hours, and yet she had an almost primeval energy.

"How long are you home for?" Vera called after their retreating backs.

Dana turned to her aunt. "Several weeks, then I am off to Greece. I have some exciting news to tell you, but later. I want to say hi first." Jackie noticed that Dana's green eyes crackled with energy as she looked at her.

Jackie stiffened when she heard the examining room door open and watched as Carin stepped outside. Dana let her arm drop down at her side. "The doctor will be with you in a few minutes," the nurse said to the room behind her.

"Carin," Vera called to the nurse. "Miss Danforth has just arrived. Should I send her back?"

"Please." Carin smiled at Jackie and turned away from Dana. She walked toward the reception area. "Hope you have a nice visit," she mumbled.

"Thank you." Dana smiled at her aunt and then turned to Jackie and winked. Dana stepped inside Jackie's office and pulled her in behind her. "I've missed you." Dana said quietly.

Jackie's knees trembled as Dana's womanly smells enveloped her. Her mouth sought Dana's, and passion climbed upward from her toes.

As her tongue sought Dana's, her hands caressed her

lover's back. Submerged passion overwhelmed her, and she reached down and pulled Dana's hips tightly against her. Her hands caressed the soft and familiar mounds, then pressed Dana against the door. Their kiss was familiar, demanding, reclaiming all those kisses of the past.

"I was so disappointed when I called the airport and they said your plane had been delayed." Jackie breathed against her lips.

"Me too. If we keep going," Dana said breathlessly against Jackie's neck, "I'm going to say the hell with your patients."

"I know."

Jackie closed her eyes and tried to ignore the ringing telephone.

"I have a feeling that's my aunt." Dana stroked Jackie's cheek. "She's doing her best to interrupt discreetly."

"I know. But I'm afraid if I let go" — Jackie looked deep into Dana's eyes — "you'll vanish again."

"I'm not going anywhere, except home, into the bathtub and then into bed. Waiting for you."

Jackie stepped back. She still felt a quaking in her legs. She picked up the telephone. "Yes?" she paused and looked at Dana, her cheeks flushed from the passion of their kiss. "I'll be right there."

Dana stepped forward and kissed Jackie lightly on the mouth. "See you tonight," she said quietly, sliding her hands up Jackie's shoulders and pulling her fervently against her. She kissed Jackie deeply, their tongues a familiar courtship. "I love you."

"I love you." Jackie shook her head as she looked at her lover. "You turn my sanity into insanity."

"Good. I plan to do that for the next few weeks."

Jackie frowned. "I don't want to think about your leaving again."

Dana held up a finger to quiet her lover. "We won't think about anything except this." Dana reached down and stroked

Jackie's breast. "And this." She let her tongue trace the outside of Jackie's ear. Jackie shivered. "That's all we'll think about."

"God, I love you." Jackie said, her mind a whitecap of passion.

"What time do you expect to be home?"

Jackie had to concentrate as she looked at the clock over her desk. "I have to make rounds, around six."

Dana gave her a puckish grin. "Good. I'll be waiting." She stepped forward and kissed Jackie on the lips and opened the door.

Carin, who was escorting young Billy Ferguson to an examining room, looked up as the door opened and again looked Dana up and down. A model's body, that was what her lover had, Jackie thought. Long legs and a thin waist that traveled up to a beautiful face.

"See you tonight," Dana said quietly.

"Hey, Doc" — Billy Ferguson held up his bandaged hand — "Mom brought me back to see you."

Jackie smiled at Billy. "Does it still hurt?"

"Heck, no. I just come cause Mom said I can't play baseball till you say it's okay." Billy shifted impatiently behind Carin.

"I'll put him in room three,'" Carin said to Jackie. "Come on, Billy. Let's get you ready for the doctor." Carin opened the examining door and motioned Billy inside.

"Thank you." Jackie ran her hand through her auburn hair as she tried to reclaim her professionalism. "See you tonight," she whispered to Dana.

Dana smiled. "Can't wait." She pressed two fingers against her lips and touched Jackie's cheek. "We may have to talk about staffing. Black hair, brown eyes, a great figure, and a Southern drawl, that's a lot of packaging," she quietly teased as she looked at the door Carin had just closed behind her.

"Never." Jackie looked into emerald eyes. "Never."

Dana laughed luxuriously. "I know that. That's what makes this so wonderful."

Jackie watched Dana walk down the hall and heard only muffled words as Dana spoke with her aunt. Jackie inhaled deeply. A trace of Dana's perfume lingered behind. Anticipation of what lay ahead that night made her feel all liquidy. She shook her head. But for now, she thought as she buttoned her white lab coat, she would have to focus on burned hands and sick bodies.

Jackie looked up at the clock. Four P.M. Four more patients and she was out the door. She picked up the chart outside the examining room and frowned when she saw the name on it. She opened the chart and looked down at the cover sheet Carin had filled out. Pulse and BP normal. Temperature fine. Jackie looked at the line reason to see the doctor, but nothing was written in the space. She knocked softly on the door before stepping inside. Jennifer Ogden was leaning against the examining table, reading a magazine. "Hi, Jackie." Jennifer smiled.

Jackie closed the door behind her. "This is a pleasant surprise."

"I see that frown. I'm not sick, everything is fine. I needed to talk privately with you, and I figured this was the best way."

Jackie set the chart on the examining table and looked at Jennifer. "Dana's home."

"Oh, Jackie," Jennifer hugged her friend. "I'm so glad. For how long? The four of us will have to get together for dinner." Jennifer paused. "But of course after you two have some time together," she added gently.

"It's just good to have her home. It's funny . . . each trip makes the loneliness just that much harder." Jackie held up her hands. "This is silly, I'm talking to you about me, and we need to talk about you. Why are you here?"

"Not so silly. We're friends. What's important to you is important to me. Dana so loves being a photojournalist."

"I know." Jackie's mind drifted as she thought about yet one more trip to the airport, putting Dana on yet another plane as she flew off to some exotic spot. Jackie felt as if she were playing a part in a continuous-loop film. "Let's talk about you."

Jennifer ignored the examining table and sat down in the chair opposite Jackie. "I am so excited." Jennifer jumped up and started pacing around the small room. " I need your help."

Jackie waited patiently.

Jennifer looked directly at her. "I want to have a baby," she announced solemnly. She sat back down in the chair again, "I — want — to — have — a — baby." She said more slowly.

"That's wonderful," Jackie smiled back. "Have you talked this over with Kristan?"

"Absolutely. We've talked about this hundreds of times. She's just as excited as I am."

"I'm glad." Jackie watched as Jennifer's eyes glowed. "But why isn't she here?"

"I wanted to surprise her."

"Jennifer, this isn't like adopting a puppy," Jackie said solemnly. "We all need to sit down and talk about medical issues. There is a wonderful woman doctor in Boston, the best in the field of artificial insemination." Jackie paused. "I assume that's what we're talking about."

"Of course." Jennifer jumped up again and started pacing around the office. "I just . . ." She stopped. "You're right. Kristan should be here with me. I've just been so excited about surprising her, I didn't think about this. Besides" — she pushed her long brown hair behind her ear — "I just wanted to make sure that my best friend and my doctor was with me on this."

"Absolutely." Jackie smiled and took off her glasses, placing them on the table. She could feel Jennifer's energy. "I think we need to start with the three of us sitting down and talking. We can do that here, but I would prefer someplace else." She chewed on the inside of her cheek. "Your house? This is too clinic-y for friends."

"Great." Jennifer hugged Jackie. "Let me know when. I don't want to get in the middle of that mush-blush stuff you'll be doing for the next few days."

"Few days? Try a few weeks."

"Right. I forget you two spend so many months apart that each return trip must feel like a honeymoon."

"Something like that," Jackie said shyly.

"Look, I've waited this long, a few more weeks won't seem like an eternity."

"We can do it sooner than that. Dana is going to want to go to Portland to visit with her family. I'll beg off and we can sit down and talk."

"Don't do that. God, I don't want to get in the way of even a minute of your time together."

"It's okay." Jackie said gently. "This is very important." She smiled mischievously. "Besides, I've never been an aunt before and am rather looking forward to it."

"Godmother," Jennifer interrupted gleefully.

"I would be honored."

"It's funny . . . when I fell in love with Kristan, I felt so lucky to be loved by that woman. But later I realized I was doubly lucky because I also got the neatest friend." She hugged Jackie again. "Give my love to Dana. Call us when you're ready for company. Promise?"

"Agreed." Jackie hesitated. "And promise me one thing."

"Absolutely."

"Tell Kristan you were here and tell her what we talked about."

"Of course, silly. I was planning on telling her anyway. I just wanted to get some of the fact-finding stuff out of the way first. You know Kristan, a typical newswoman, don't bother her with the minuscule when she prefers to have the whole story."

"But she would be hurt if you left her out of this part."
Jennifer folded her hands in front of her. "You're right. I was so wrapped up in wanting to surprise her that I was being selfish." Jennifer cocked her head as she thought about what she had done. She hooked her arm through Jackie's and opened the door to the examining room. "Come on, Doc, time for you to see your last few patients and go home."

"No argument here." Jackie stopped in front of the examining room where she knew Mrs. Clark would be waiting. "See you soon."

"Promise. Call when you're ready for company. In the meantime, I'll talk with Kristan. She's going to be as excited as I am."

Jackie's Mustang seemed to be on autopilot as it turned toward her home. Her tires spun on the gravel in her driveway. Dana's rental car was parked in front of the garage. A vassal to routine, Jackie usually put her car in the garage before going into the house, but not tonight. She parked next to Dana's rental, reached across the seat for her black bag, and quick stepped to the open front door. Without a word they kissed.

"When did you get this?" Dana reached behind her and picked up a puppy.

"A few weeks ago." Jackie kissed her again, the puppy struggling between them as it tried to lick Jackie's face. "I came home from work, and she walked out from behind one of the maple trees. She was dragging her left back leg, her fur was dirty and matted, and she was an absolute mess." Jackie said between kisses. "But when she looked at me with those pathetic eyes and whimpered, I was a goner. I called Kristan, and she got the vet to make a house call. Anyway, the vet examined her and found that her back leg was hurt, not broken. She cleaned her up and, well, here she is."

"It was so weird because this woman dropped her off just a little while ago, I thought she had the wrong driveway."

"That's Kathy. She runs the day-care center for dogs."

"Day-care?"

Jackie blushed. "Kinda foolish. I don't like her being alone." Jackie looked wistfully at the puppy. "And because I didn't want anything to interfere with our first few seconds together tonight, I called Kathy and asked her to drop her off."

"She's adorable." Dana gave Jackie an amused look as she rubbed her face against the puppy's soft fur. The puppy nuzzled Dana's cheek. "What did you name her?"

"Bob."

Dana looked at Jackie as if she had said a foreign word. "Bob. You named a little girl puppy *Bob*? You couldn't tell the difference between a little girl and little boy puppy? It's a good thing you're not a vet," Dana teased.

Jackie reached out and stroked Bob's head. The puppy struggled to get free of Dana and into the arms of her owner. "I didn't really look, and *Bob* just kind of popped into my head."

"Bob." Dana handed the still struggling puppy to Jackie. "She adores you."

The puppy put her tiny paws against Jackie's shoulder and snuggled against her neck. "Me neither." Jackie looked down at the pup. "She's kinda spoiled."

"Good, and I'll spoil her and her owner even more." Dana traced a finger up Jackie's arm.

Jackie put Bob on the floor and handed her her chew toy. The puppy tossed the tiny rubber bone in the air. "Here ya go, little guy. Right now you're in the way." Jackie drew Dana close until their bodies touched. She kissed Dana's lips, a gentle, tender kiss that communicated the longing she had felt while Dana was gone. She took Dana's hand and led her to their bedroom.

As she untied the string on Dana's robe and kissed each

patch of bare skin, she was intoxicated by her scent. Jackie marveled that she had survived without it for so long. Their first few minutes together was always the same. Jackie felt shy, trapped in a state of colossal confusion, but behind that was a primal need to be as close to Dana as she possibly could. Jackie clung to Dana, her trembling betraying her fear that her lover might simply melt away. It had been three months since they had been together, and all the romantic fantasies she had harbored while Dana was away erupted. No dreams tonight, she thought as they kissed. Jackie looked deep into Dana's eyes and saw a volcano that matched her passion. She yanked off her own shirt.

"I need a shower," she whispered.

"Later," Dana said against her lips.

Jackie's skin felt on fire. Dana's hand reached up behind her back and unsnapped Jackie's bra. Jackie impatiently shrugged the straps from around her shoulders, their breasts touching and then folding into one another, their warmth and softness seeking heat.

Jackie eased her tongue deep into Dana's mouth. She began to lick and suck Dana's lips as if she had to consume them. The heat of Dana's skin bathed her throat, shoulders, and arms.

As she pushed Dana back on the bed, Jackie thought about what Dana had told her after the first time they had made love. She said she considered lovemaking the ultimate communication of trust, the gift of one's body to a lover with absolute confidence that only goodness and pleasure would result.

Jackie felt the response of Dana's body, and felt Dana draw in her breath as her hand reached to touch Dana's waist. She knelt over Dana and kissed and sucked her breast. She savored the scent of bath soap and the salty taste of her skin. Her lips sought the sweetness of Dana's breast, and she gently drew as much as she could her mouth. Jackie felt a pulsing between her thighs.

Dana groaned. "God I've missed you." She pulled Jackie to her and crushed her in her arms.

"I don't ever want you to go again," Jackie whispered. She was frightened by the fear that now consumed her, the fear she felt each time Dana came home, because each return meant another leaving.

"I love you," Dana kissed Jackie. "I want you."

Jackie responded with a deep long kiss. She stroked Dana's breast, then traced a line along Dana's thigh and felt a tremor like the sensation one gets when touching a railroad track. Dana reached down and pushed at the top of Jackie's slacks. " I want to feel you against me," Dana said. Jackie rolled over, unzipped her pants, and kicked them onto the floor. She slipped out of her panties and then rolled back onto her lover. Her tongue trailed downward toward Dana's stomach.

Dana raised up on her elbows. "Let me, I want to touch you."

Jackie couldn't stop. "Later." As her tongue kept up the same rhythm and she licked just below Dana's navel, she marveled at how she had existed for three months without the closeness of this woman. And at the same time she sensed the blackness that would envelop her if Dana were to leave forever. She slowly eased the panties over Dana's hips. Her tongue followed the movement downward. Then she reached the spot she had dreamed of for so many nights. She felt the rawness of Dana's passion and the synchrony of their two bodies moving together.

It is now, Jackie thought, now that she had to draw Dana into a closeness that neither of them would ever want to leave. But in the back of her mind, an apparition of dread began to loom.

Dana moaned deep in her throat. "Oh yes."

Jackie's tongue stroked back and forth, light and hard, up and down, each move calculated to bring pleasure rather than climax. As Jackie teased the flower open before her, she realized that she was in danger. She knew that, like the sailors in the *Odyssey*, if she ate of this lotus she would never be satisfied with anything else. Then she lowered her head to Dana and consumed her. In a few moments they both were rocked by Dana's passionate explosion.

Jackie collapsed next to her on the bed, feverish and scorched by the fire of their lovemaking. But she was also chilled by the irrational possibility that this might be the last time they made love. She did not know when Dana would leave again, but she knew it would be soon.

Dana touched Jackie's breasts, her voice smoked with passion. "I've missed touching you." She pulled Jackie to her and laid her on her back. She pressed her knee between Jackie's thighs and sucked first one and then the other of Jackie's nipples. The perspiration produced by Jackie's vigorous effort had gathered under her breasts, and it was Dana's turn to savor the salty flavor of love. As Dana stroked her gently with her fingertips, it was Jackie's turn to tremble.

Twined in each other's arms, Dana nuzzled closer to Jackie. "I miss this almost as much as the lovemaking."

"Me too." Funny, she thought. She felt so alive when their bodies were touching. "This bed feels so big when you're not here."

Dana leaned her head on her hand and stared down at Jackie. "I suspect now that you have Bob, you'll have few empty-bed nights."

Jackie gazed raptly into Dana's eyes. "No way. I already told Bob that she sleeps on the floor next to our bed." Jackie said. "Although," she grinned sheepishly, "she's so little that I do cuddle her a lot. And she really does like day care."

"Day care," Jackie watched as Dana shook her head again as she tried to accustom herself to the word.

"Yeah," Jackie said, her cheeks a rich scarlet. She wasn't

sure how to describe how lonely she felt when she left Bob alone. Jackie understood alone. "I drop her off in the morning and pick her up in the evening. It works out quite well. She gets to visit with her canine pals."

Dana smirked. "Day care. Although . . . ?"

Jackie studied her lover's face. She loved the way Dana's eyebrow arched when she was mulling over a problem. "Although?"

"Well, I was going to save this until later, but I'm just too excited." Dana sat crossed legged on the bed. "I've been offered something very exciting and although at first I was going to turn it down, I was able to negotiate some things and, well —"

"And, well?" Jackie repeated quietly. She could feel the tension in her stomach, uncertain what this latest announcement would mean to their lives.

"I've been offered a three-year photojournalist assignment in Greece working exclusively for their largest magazine. That means no more running around the world and, the best part, I negotiated for a house and you can live there with me. I checked with the consulate. Although there will be some hoops to jump through, you can practice medicine there. We'd be in the Land of Lesbos." Dana's face was flushed from their lovemaking and her excitement.

Jackie leaned up on her elbows. "Three years in Greece?"

"Yes, but you didn't hear the best part. You can be there with me. No more two months together and then off on another shoot. This is three years together," she added quickly.

Dana's words seemed overpowering to Jackie. "We've never talked about my leaving. I've never thought about not being at the clinic."

"But that's the best part — this is not forever. And you'd be back in three years. This would give you a chance to do other things in medicine. You've talked about wanting to do other things."

Jackie swung her legs to the side of the bed. "That's just talk after a hard day. Everyone has their flash of should-would-coulda, but that doesn't mean what if ever comes."

"But it has come, darling. We've talked about being together all the time," Dana touched Jackie's arm.

"I meant when you retire. I was willing to put up with this fractured schizophrenic personal life because I thought someday you would tire of the travel and want to settle down here." Jackie emphasized here with her index finger. "I thought you'd want to finish that photojournalism book you started. Honest, Dana, I never even considered that I'd be the one to leave." Jackie suddenly felt weary.

"Don't you want to be with me?"

"Don't do that." Jackie held up her hand as if to accentuate the silence. "You know I want to be with you every moment of our lives." She gazed intently into her lover's eyes and wondered if Dana knew how expressive they were. "I love you. You're the first woman since Marianne died of cancer who has filled every space in my mind, soul, and heart." Jackie paused. "I just never thought about leaving the clinic for that long a period of time." Jackie stood up. "I don't know, I just don't know."

Dana reached for her robe. "I'm sorry."

Jackie saw the tears in her eyes, but felt too paralyzed to reach out to her.

"I shouldn't have brought this up my first night home. But I was just so damned excited. I don't know" — Jackie watched as she pushed her red hair still damp from their lovemaking off her forehead — "I'm sorry, truly sorry." She reached out a hand to Jackie.

Jackie entwined her fingers in Dana's. "And I'm sorry for reacting like I did. I just never expected —"

Dana took Jackie in her arms. "I know. The idea takes getting used to. Would you just think about it." Dana held up a hand. "Just consider the possibility. Another country, a different kind of medicine and I'm not talking about practicing at a hospital for the rich, but doing the kind of medicine you love most. Just think about it, please? And . . ." Dana smiled. "You can bring Bob."

Jackie laughed. "I'll think about it. I owe it to us to do that much." Jackie reached for her robe. "Come on, I'll make us a scrambled egg sandwich."

Dana grinned. "Never let it be said that I don't have a knack for taking away the warm afterglow of love. Come on." She tied the strings on Jackie's robe. "I'll make the toast."

Chapter 2

Joni slipped her shoe off and rubbed the bottom of her foot against her leg. She was worn out. The patients had been nonstop and spring colds and flu topped the chart of patient complaints. She leaned her head back and closed her eyes. This was going to be a short lunch break. She opened her eyes as the door to the lounge opened.

"You look as tuckered as a lobster being tossed about in a storm," Carin said as she stepped into the employees' lounge. They had been hired within days of each other in February, and Joni knew Carin was dancing around the edge of friendship.

"A little." Joni picked up the coffeepot and poured. She studied the inside of her mug. "I know this was just made this morning, but why does it look like something that escaped from a Florida swamp?"

Carin leaned over and looked inside the cup. "It looks more like something you should rub on a chest for a cold rather than something you should drink." She set her lunch on the table.

"That's what I'm afraid of." Joni took a tentative sip and screwed up her face. "You have to love coffee to drink this stuff."

Carin laughed. "I have an extra can of juice in the refrigerator; it's yours. My husband packed my lunch today, and he forgets he's sending off a nurse, not an over-the-road truck driver."

"Thanks, but I find drinking this an adventure. Plus, it's going to keep me not only awake, but probably wired."

Carin's laugh was involuntary. She held up her sandwich. "Would you like half?"

"Thanks, I brought a salad."

"I love salads. 'Course I don't have to watch my weight like you, so I don't eat as many. Probably should, though." Carin bit into her sandwich. "By the way, you've never said if someone's home fixing your salads?"

Joni hesitated. She was sensitive about her weight, but she also had learned in the past few weeks that Carin rarely realized when she had tripped into a sensitive area. This was not the first time Carin had poked and probed.

"Significant other? I think that's what they call it nowadays?" Carin chewed on her sandwich.

Joni concentrated on cutting her lettuce and took a bite. She knew Carin was desperate for a friend. But Joni's alarm had kicked in soon after they had started working together, and she had decided there would be no personal tidbits of life. Carin oozed gossip. She recalled the day after one of the doctor's friends had visited. Carin was absolutely animated as she talked about the woman's fiery hair and clothes. "I live alone," Joni said.

"After nursing school" — Carin bit into her sandwich — "I lived alone for exactly two months, and then Darrel came along. We met at a bar in Atlanta. God, he was gorgeous. Black hair, small hips. It was l-o-v-e at first nibble." Carin giggled at her own joke.

Joni smiled.

"We've been married five years."

"No children?" Joni decided to dump the questions back in Carin's lap.

"No, we have to wait. Darrel wants to build up his plumbing and heating business. He's from here, been away a long time. So it's like starting over," Carin paused and took another bite of her sandwich. "I'm not sure I'm going to like the winters." Her Southern voice dripped with doubt. "Somehow I think that's when I'm going to miss Atlanta the most. But I like the clinic. Jackie is so easy to work for, and Vera is such a peach."

Both women heard the handle turn. Vera smiled at the two women. "I wish I had good news," she said as she retrieved a bottle of iced tea from the refrigerator. "But the hospital just called, and Jackie had to rush over there because of an emergency. It looks like we're going to be stacking the afternoon patients in the rooms and in the reception area until she gets back."

Both Carin and Joni groaned.

"I'd better call my husband and tell him he's going to be cooking again tonight. Why don't you sit a minute. Ya look beat," Carin said.

Vera rubbed the back of her neck. "I've got only a minute." She sipped her iced tea. "I know as sure as I'm here that the minute I start to relax someone will come in early for their appointment."

"By the way, I didn't get to tell you what a lovely niece you have," Carin said.

Joni looked down at her salad; she knew Carin had been drooling for this moment.

"Thank you. Dana is very special."

"What does she do?" Carin persisted.

"She's a photojournalist. She travels all over the world. I think she is headed to Greece next." Vera frowned. "Yes, I think that's what she told me. She has the life most women only dream about. You've seen her pictures in *Time* and *Newsweek*. But as she says, nobody but another photojournalist pays attention to who took the picture."

"Wow, that sounds so neat. A career to die for, gorgeous red hair, and a figure that would make most men dribble saliva and women turn green with envy. Well, most women," she quickly added.

Joni smothered a smile. She knew Carin considered her own slender frame something to die for. She listened as Carin skillfully tried to turn the questioning to a more intimate path.

"Have she and Jackie been friends long?"

Vera set her half-drunk iced tea on the table. She looked directly at Carin. "They've known each other their whole lives." Vera picked up her tea. "I guess I'd better check on the reception area."

Carin waited until Vera shut the door. "Wow, she's protective. You weren't here when the niece stopped by the office. I can tell you, she was only in with the doctor for about ten minutes, but when she came out, Jackie's cheeks were flaming. You could have lit a match off the broil from her cheeks, and I don't think it was because their conversation was that stimulating." Carin lowered her voice. "I think they're lesbians."

"Does that bother you?"

"Hell no, this is the millennium. When I told Darrel, he thought it was disgusting. Wanted me to quit in a minute. Said the doctor would be hitting on me every second." Carin laughed alone. "I told him I was a big girl and no one was going to take advantage of me. Besides" — Carin winked conspiratorially — "I am not into women and, I didn't want

21

to tell him this 'cause it would have swelled his head, but he does a good job of satisfying me at home." Carin giggled again.

Joni picked up her empty salad dish and rinsed it. Yup, she thought, she was not going to like this woman. "Well, I don't think either one of us has anything to worry about. I suspect the doctor rarely notices the women in her office."

Carin stroked strands of her hair. "Maybe, maybe not. It would be a bit of a challenge to see if you could get her to kinda look at the goods. Not that I'd ever do that. Like I said, Darrel takes good care of me at home."

Joni put her washed dishes away. She was going to ask the doctor if she and Carin could stagger their lunch hours. A book would be better than this, she thought. She wondered if she should check to see if there were any openings at the hospital.

Chapter 3

Vera stepped into Jackie's office and laid a stack of telephone messages on her desk. Jackie did not look up from *The Merck Manual.* "Two more patients, I let Carin go home. She and her husband are celebrating their fifth anniversary." Vera paused. "They're going to spend the night swinging with the monkeys at the zoo and then going to eat stuffed ostrich under glass. She obviously needed to leave a little earlier, what with swinging monkeys and ostrich under glass —"

Jackie laid the manual down and sorted through the messages. "Fine," she said distractedly. She noted the message from her friend Kristan.

"You're not listening."

Jackie looked up and smiled at her long-time friend. When

Jackie and Marianne, who was a nurse, had started the practice they had hired Vera as their receptionist. Eventually Vera had taken over the day-to-day operation of the clinic but had insisted on remaining her receptionist. Eventually, the practice had grown and Jackie opened a clinic. Jackie suspected Vera liked the one-on-one meeting with patients more than anything else. She knew everyone in Bailey's Cove. Jackie had long days, but she knew Vera's were even longer. At the end of the day Vera carried home accounting ledgers. "You're right."

Vera hesitated, her hand on the door. "I let Carin go early. She and her husband are celebrating their anniversary, dinner the whole bit. Or, as she says, *a night you'd like to die for,*" Vera mimicked. When Jackie did not respond, Vera sat down. "Dana told me."

Jackie shook her head. "Total life decisions."

"I've known you forever." Vera smoothed the edges of her dress. "And nothing I say will help solve this, but promise me one thing . . . Do what makes you happy, not what you think will make Dana happy."

"That's not as easy as it sounds. Dana makes me happy." Jackie laid her glasses on her desk and pushed a frustrated palm through her hair.

"I know. But think of your life as a painted picture. Dana is just one color."

Jackie smiled. "It sounds like you've been thinking about this. Are you trying to convince me not to go?"

"I'm trying to convince you to do what makes you happy. Even if it means eliminating that one color from your palette for a while. And I say that even though I love my niece very much. She's been here four weeks, and she knows you well. She's worried you don't want to go. She called me before she left. I know she's in New York finalizing the Greece trip. She tried to pump me for information, but I told her we hadn't even talked about the move, which until this very moment was true."

"She wanted me to go to New York with her," Jackie blurted out. "But I couldn't, Vera. I knew as well as I'm sitting here that I couldn't go, and I can't figure out why. It was just for a few days. I felt" — Jackie pushed both hands through her hair — "that if I went to New York, I'd never come back. I don't want to hurt Dana." Jackie gulped back the fear she had been feeling.

"Then don't go. Dana will be hurt, but she's a survivor. She loves you, but she loves what she does more. Dana overdoses on the assignment. She's an adrenaline junky, and each new photo shoot feeds that high. Trying to get a hold of her at those times is like trying to write on water," Vera paused to let her words sink in. "You've seen her when she's left here; she's flying, and I don't mean that literally."

Jackie touched her index finger to her lips. "That's what I've been too afraid to articulate. I also realized, Vera, that I love what I do, but I love it because it happens here." Jackie pointed at her desk as if it was the entire clinic. "What I'm battling is, do I love it more than I love Dana?"

"Maybe you do, but so what? I told you I love Dana, but it would be cruel to both of you if you went somewhere you didn't want to be. You'd end up hating your job and Dana. And somehow, although Dana's going to be hurt, better now than later when the hurt could turn into bitter words between you. Or worse, just left to fester." Vera stood up. "Jackie, you're a surgeon. You need to excise the problem now, not later."

"Dana gets home Monday. Two days are going to feel like a lifetime."

"You're not on call this weekend; go for a hike. Better yet, take Bob for a walk on the beach. Go bother Kristan. But just stop thinking about it for a while. Promise?"

"Promise," Jackie sighed.

"Good." Vera hesitated at the opened door. "Jackie, Dana is lovingly incorrigible. Don't let her intensity swallow you up. Don't back down from this. You know in your soul that your going isn't going to work. Now just say the words."

Jackie clasped her hands together and rested her chin on her fingers after Vera left. The weeks had disappeared quickly after Dana had told her. They had discussed the job in Greece, the people she would be working with, and the opportunities Dana said would be there for her. But not whether Jackie would be joining her. Memorial Day they had walked on the beach. Made love to the sound of crashing waves. At night Dana had been an exercise in restraint, and those hours they made love seemed to resolve everything. But then morning would come and with it the depression. She could feel it nibbling at her vitality. She wasn't a clinical psychologist, but she knew that this depth of depression would consume her and only she could stop it. Outwardly her life seemed normal. Well, almost normal. She had suffered these emotions before.

When Marianne's breast cancer had come back two years after she was first diagnosed, Marianne had demanded Jackie not stay at home but go into the clinic. She kept telling her she wanted at least that part of their life to be normal. Her lover knew that only work would help Jackie get through what was going to happen next. Marianne had been a nurse and had shared Jackie's passion for what they did. But then Marianne had died, and for years Jackie had been alone with only her work to challenge her. During those long weeks while Jackie stayed with Marianne at the hospital in Bangor, Vera and Kristan had been her grappling iron, helping her get through those days when Marianne died. Then after years alone, she'd met Dana. Jackie dropped her head on her chest and rubbed her temples. She felt like she was in the middle of a Harlequin Romance. She should be willing to toss away everything for her lover, but she couldn't. And that was the threadbare truth she had been refusing to say out loud. She glanced down at her messages. She frowned when she saw that this was Kristan's third telephone call that day. She wondered how her longtime friend had responded to Jennifer's news. She reached for the telephone.

"Excuse me, Doctor?"

Jackie jumped. She had not heard Joni open the door. "Yes?" She dropped the receiver back onto its cradle.

"I'm sorry." Joni smiled. "I did knock, I just thought you'd like to know —"

"I know, I have patients waiting." Jackie buttoned her white coat. "This can wait." She laid Kristan's message back on her desk. "Let's get to it. And behind door number one is who?" Jackie smiled at her nurse. She liked Joni's quiet attentiveness to duty. Her résumé had been solid. Like Jackie, she had been at Massachusetts General Hospital for a while before returning home. Joni was younger than Jackie was, so they had not known each other in grade school. Jackie had been a senior in high school when Joni was a freshman.

Joni chuckled. "Mrs. Rogers. She has the flu."

"And behind door number two?"

"Little Jimmy Carver."

"Ah yes, the broken arm. I expect there's no one behind door three because I vaguely remember Vera's saying something about only two patients left."

"Right. Two patients, hospital rounds, and then you are out of here for the weekend. I told Vera to go home. I can lock up."

"Good, then let's get to it."

They moved through the next two patients with ease. Antibiotics for Mrs. Rogers and a tiny celebration with the removal of Jimmy's cast. Jackie had cut around the scribbled messages from his friends.

Jackie rubbed her hand against the back of her neck and stretched. Joni was cleaning up the examining room. "Long day. And I still have rounds to make."

"Don't you wish some days you could just walk away from all the stress?"

Jackie hesitated.

"I'm sorry, Doctor. I overstepped. I meant," Joni stopped. "I meant —"

"No apology needed. I didn't see it as —" Jackie heard the pounding on the outside door and the muffled "Help me, help me." She also could hear the choked cries and screams of a child.

"Come on," she said as she ran up the hallway. Jackie unlocked the outside door and saw Jenny Bagley, her son Tommy twisting in her arms. His face was covered in blood, which was dripping onto Jenny's coat

"It just happened. He stumbled getting out of the car and hit his head."

Tommy was screaming.

"Follow me," Jackie ordered.

Joni ran ahead to the examining room and was pulling out gauze pads and antiseptics as Jackie entered.

While Jackie cleaned the wound, Joni spoke gently to Tommy. Jackie watched as Joni stroked his cheek with the back of her hand.

"It's not that serious," Jackie said as she checked his eyes and felt for other bumps. "He's going to have a small L-shaped scar though," Jackie assured the mother. "Two tiny stitches and he'll be fine. A small headache, but fine."

"God, I got so scared." Jenny sniffled. "All that blood. I thought he had a concussion or something."

Jackie talked quietly as she anesthetized the area. "Hey, big guy. This is going to hurt a little, but not as much as hitting your head. I need to fix that cut, okay?" Tommy shook his head up and down. His brown eyes seemed unusually large in his pale face. "And when we're done, I'm going to give you a big sucker. Which would you prefer, red, purple, orange, yellow?" Jackie worked quickly.

"Red." Tommy said between little whimpers.

"Good choice. That's my favorite color too. They're all done." Joni handed Jackie the gauze pad and tape. Jackie smiled. "Thank you." Oblivious of the blood, she reached down and picked Tommy up in her arms. "Now, let's me and you go in search of that sucker, maybe even two suckers, while the nurse helps Mom clean up. Okay?"

Tommy looked back at his mother. "Okay."

"You were great." Jackie said to Joni later. Tommy and his mother had left, and Joni was cleaning the examining room. "I could tell you had been a surgical nurse before," Jackie studied the woman's face. "You anticipated my every move."

"Early on I was a surgical nurse, but got out of it."

"Why? I have a feeling you were very good."

"The stress. More and varied surgeries. Working with doctors who yelled at you when they made a mistake. The usual."

"You're very good," Jackie said matter-of-factly. "How about your letting me buy you a cup of tea? I have some excellent herbal teas in my office."

Joni smiled. "Thanks. I'd like that. Just let me finish here."

Jackie went into the lounge and put two cups of water in the microwave. She carried the steaming cups into her office and searched through her credenza for boxes of tea.

Joni tapped quietly on the open door.

"Come in." She held up several boxes. "I have mint, cherry, ginkgo sharp, and, of course, tension tamer."

Joni smiled. "Mint, please."

"Good choice. I'll join you." She put tea bags in each cup and handed the cup and a spoon to Joni. "Milk? Sugar?"

"Nope, I take my tea straight up."

"A purist. Me too. Please sit." Jackie gestured at a chair near her desk. Jackie studied the other woman over her teacup. Joni was attractive in a quiet way. She had dark brown hair and, Jackie noticed for the first time, honey brown eyes. Where Dana was tall and angular, Joni was petite and round. "Do you regret leaving the big city of Boston for the Down East area?" Jackie said to break the silence.

"Just sometimes." Joni sipped her tea. "How do I explain it . . . I'm glad I came back, but there are parts of my life there that I miss. My friends, the theater, the Boston Symphony, and" — Joni chuckled — "I'm a closet baseball fan, so I do miss the occasional Red Sox game. They never fail to disappoint me."

Jackie laughed. "After I moved here, I followed their games for a while. But most of the time I found myself mad. So I stopped watching and listening. Although I do miss going to a game."

"I not only miss the game, but the steamed soggy hot dogs and spilled beer."

"Right, I forgot," Jackie laughed.

"But I've adapted. Now I take long walks along the ocean or ski at the Moosehorn National Wildlife Refuge."

"If I remember, you were in the process of buying a home soon after you arrived. I remember Vera saying something about that."

"Yes, not far from you. I bought the old Gardner house."

"That's right." Jackie set her cup on her desk. "I was in there many times as a kid."

"It needs a lot of work, but I like it. In Boston I owned a home in the city. I'd sneeze and my neighbor would say God bless you." Joni shrugged. "You get the idea."

Jackie held up a hand. "You don't have to explain. Houses so close together you can smell your neighbor's breakfast bacon. I know exactly what you mean. For years I lived in townhouses and hated it. I knew I was not cut out for community living, so I never bought a house. A house would have made my stay there a lot more permanent."

"It did for me." Joni sipped her tea. "But I just decided to dump the house. I was lucky, sold it soon after I had it on the market. And I'm glad I'm back. I understand . . . you gave up some promising offers to come home."

Jackie rested her chin on her thumb. "I think the word *promising* is slightly exaggerated. I did turn down some job offers, but you used the right word, this was *home*. I started with a small office. The first person I hired was Vera. Now we have the clinic, and with the increasing workload I'm seriously considering adding another doctor. Although —" Jackie stopped. "I probably shouldn't announce that quite yet because I haven't told Vera. She'd tear a seam if she knew I was adding someone without first consulting her. She's the boss, chief, you name it, and every once in a while she reminds me. So before I'd even think about hiring another doctor, I'm going to tell her. She likes being part of the interview process. Says she's a better arbiter of character than I am." Jackie smiled.

Joni laughed. "I won't tell her. I'm not about to upset someone with that much power," Joni teased. "But I hope that a new doctor doesn't mean you're thinking of leaving."

Jackie was drawn to Joni's eyes. There was an innate gentleness. "I'm struggling with a proposal. Some would call it an opportunity, but . . . I haven't made a final decision." Jackie did a quick reprise in her mind of her conversation with Vera.

"Well." Joni set her empty cup on the desk. "I've been there before. I'm not going to ask you what it is you're grappling with, but I do hope that whatever the decision is, your choice makes you more than fifty percent happy."

"Now that's an interesting way of putting it. Not one hundred percent happy?"

"I don't know. I think as an adult you never quite reach one hundred percent in anything. There are just too many compromises, too many other people to consider. Heck, I'm satisfied if I achieve contentment, forget happiness."

"You're right. Although . . ." Jackie said more to herself than to Joni. "If I chose leaving, I would make someone else one hundred percent happy."

"Then that is something you have to factor in. But you have to decide if you can live off of that other person's happiness. I've found in my life, anyway, that just doesn't work." The door chimed and Joni frowned. "In the confusion, I may not have locked that door." She stood up and turned toward the hall. "But I thought I checked it after Mrs. Bagley left." She stopped when she saw Carin in the hallway.

"I didn't expect to find you still here." Jackie heard the surprise in Carin's voice. "I saw the light and wondered if the doctor was still here."

Jackie stepped from behind Joni. "Still here. Is there something you wanted?"

"Well, as a matter of fact" — Carin looked from Joni to the doctor — "I was wondering if you'd like to come to supper sometime. I just thought it'd be nice if Darrel, that's my husband, 'course you knew that." Carin's giggle sounded tense. "I thought it'd be nice if we got to know you. I told Darrel and he said you'd not want to hang around with the petite bourgeoisie. That man," she laughed again. "Gets those big words off television, I'd just like to die."

"Well, thank you, and tell Darrel thanks for the invitation. I would love to come to dinner some night."

"Great! That would be just great!" Carin started to back down the hallway. "Maybe you could join us Joni. I know Darrel would just love to meet you. I've told him all about you and how we're getting to be just great friends."

"Thank you." Jackie noticed Joni had stopped short of accepting.

"I've got to get going." Carin turned to leave, then turned around again. "We're celebrating our anniversary, and Darrel just hates to be kept waiting. I was in town buying a few things for tonight. You know," Carin stopped and added almost confidentially, "the bare essentials."

They watched as Carin chattered her way to the reception door. "Well, bye-bye." Carin called from the door. "I'll just lock this."

"What was that all about?" Jackie frowned at Joni.

"I don't know, but let me, as they say Down East, churn on it for a while."

"When you figure it out, tell me, because I sure as heck don't have a clue." Jackie looked at her watch. "Wow, I've got to make my rounds. Thank you." Jackie smiled and gestured toward the cups.

"I enjoyed it," Joni said. "Go make your rounds. I'll finish here and lock up."

Jackie noted her sudden shyness. "Thanks." Jackie reached for her coat and stepped into the hallway, then stepped back into her office. "Would you like to have dinner tonight? Dana is in New York, and I find myself free."

"Thank you, Doctor. I'd enjoy that."

"Please call me Jackie. How about seven-thirty at the Shoreside Inn?"

Joni smiled. "I'll meet you there."

"Good." Jackie smiled too. "I'm glad Carin stopped. It offered just the right impetus for me to do more than just go home. Thank you."

Chapter 4

Jackie found herself humming as she changed at the hospital. She had learned to keep a clean set of clothing in her locker for just such moments. She thought about her upcoming dinner with Joni and chuckled as she discovered she actually was looking forward to it. Jackie stopped as she tucked her shirt into her pants. She couldn't quite figure out what there was about Joni that seemed so familiar. She liked her quiet presence and sensed that Joni didn't need to always fill the air with words. She knew that Vera liked her a lot, and that was superlative evidence of her character. Vera always made it clear to Jackie whom she liked and didn't like, including Carin. Vera insisted that anyone who changed the spelling of her name from *Karen* to *Carin* was just a bit too pretentious for her liking.

Jackie remembered the rush to hire Carin. Vera was ready to leave on a cruise with her mother when their regular nurse, all tears and faced with problems with her eight-year-old son, announced that she was moving to Portland. That was months ago. Vera at first had insisted she would cancel her vacation, but Jackie had been just as insistent that she go on the cruise. So Vera found a temporary nurse, but within days of Vera's departure the temp announced she was leaving her job to go to medical school. Jackie in desperation hired Carin on the spot. She had just moved to Bailey's Cove, and her credentials seemed okay. Jackie replayed that week in her head.

She chuckled as she recalled trying to operate the clinic without an office manager or nurse. For the first time in her life, she knew exactly how Susan Sarandon had felt in *The Rocky Horror Picture Show*, as if weird things were going on around you and all you could do was stand and watch. When Vera returned she was miffed that someone had joined the clinic without her approval. A week later, Joni applied and Vera announced that she liked the woman and hired her. Jackie found that she relied more and more on Joni and realized it was because the woman had good medical instincts.

And now as she got dressed, Jackie realized she was looking forward to dinner with Joni. She looked at the clock. Eight o'clock. She mentally groused at herself; her reminiscing had used up valuable minutes. She called the day-care center to make certain that Bob could stay a few extra hours. That settled, Jackie left the hospital.

Jackie saw Joni just as she stepped in the door. Joni's face awash in candlelight was a montage of warm colors. She nodded to Jim Stevenson that she would seat herself.

"Sorry, I got delayed."

"Don't apologize," Joni smiled. "I was content to just sit here and look out at the bay. The sky was shades of pink, dark and light, intense and muted. Now a full moon rising. Who could ask for anything more perfect?"

Jackie looked out the window. "Breathtaking."

"I never tire of looking at the water. You might think this foolish . . ." Joni hesitated as if undecided how much she wished to reveal of her life. "When I lived in Boston," she began tentatively, "I could see the bay anytime, it was a car drive away. Or I could drive to Hyannis or Provincetown for the weekend, but it wasn't the same. There is something about this place that is intoxicating, and no matter how long I live I'm going to remain drunk on life in Maine. It's my bold coast romance. I am in love with the view. Does that sound daft?"

"Maybe to an outsider, but for anyone who lives here it makes absolute sense." Jackie looked up as Betty Hanes approached.

"Good evening," Betty said to Jackie.

"How are things, Betty?"

"Wonderful," Betty smiled. "Alex is growing like Jack and the Beanstalk."

"How old is he now?"

"Six months, and what a set of lungs. Bill and I decided we have a future rock star. Would you like a bottle of wine?"

"Yes." Jackie looked distractedly at the wine list. "I remember when he was this big" — Jackie held her hands close together — "he was a tiny squirt. By the way, I don't think you two know one another. This is Joni Coan, a former Bailey's Cover who's returned home and now is a nurse in our clinic. And this is Betty Hanes, the best waitress at the Seaside Inn."

"Now, Doc."

"I've made you blush. Good," Jackie teased.

"Pleased to meet you," Betty said, ignoring Jackie. "I

thought you looked familiar. I think you were in my sister's class. I used to be Betty Clark; my sister is Esther Clark, well, now Esther James," she said.

"Yes, I remember. How is your sister?"

"Great. Lives in New York. She and her husband have four children. A real handful," Betty said. "I'm sorry, I should have gotten your wine," she said to Jackie.

"Don't let me interrupt," Jackie smiled. "I know begats are important."

"Begats?" Joni said.

"You know who's related to whom. Don't let me interrupt." Jackie's smile was puckish.

"You're in a mood to tease me tonight," Betty said. "Would you like the usual?"

"Do you have a preference for wine?" Jackie asked Joni as she handed the wine list to Betty.

"As far as I'm concerned, whatever is your usual," Joni smiled. "Is fine with me."

"A bottle of Beringer's White Zinfandel."

"Coming right up and nice meeting you. I'll tell Esther I saw you."

"So." Jackie folded her fingers together. "What have you been doing since I've last seen you?"

Joni smiled. "I went home, grabbed a quick shower, and rushed right back over here. And you?"

"No complications at the hospital; rounds went smoothly. But I found myself trying to remember something."

"What?"

"There is something familiar about you; I can't put my finger on it."

Joni rested her chin on the back of her hand. "We were in two different leagues in high school. I was a clam, and you were a haddock. So I didn't think you even remembered me."

"Clam, haddock? Are we thinking of dinner?" Jackie laughed.

Joni smiled. "Probably, but you were class president, head

of the student council. Very popular in school. I used to see you in the hallway, kids schooling around you, excuse the pun. I wish I'd been a senior. I'd have hung around you too."

"Me too, then we could have been friends sooner." Jackie smiled as she toyed with the fork. "I don't even remember that as an important part of my life. What was important was college and then medical school. If anything offers a reality check on your life, that's it. Pulling all-nighters. Wondering if you'd get through school," Jackie shook her head.

"No question about that." Joni stopped as Betty set the chilled wine next to their table and poured.

"I know you haven't had a chance to look at your menus. Just give me the high sign when you're ready to order."

Jackie looked down at her unopened menu. "Thanks, Betty." Jackie lifted her glass. "To newfound friendship."

Joni clicked her glass against Jackie's. "Thank you."

They sipped their wine.

"Well, stranger."

Jackie was out of her chair when she heard the familiar voice. "Hey, buddy." She hugged the woman. "Joni, this is my friend Kristan Cassidy. Joni Coan is a nurse at the clinic." Kristan shook Joni's hand.

Jackie stepped back and looked at her friend's face and was startled at the tension she saw. Her eyes were bloodshot, her cheeks blotchy. Now she knew why there had been three telephone calls to the clinic. Jackie mentally kicked herself for not immediately responding to Kristan's calls.

"How are you?" Kristan asked Jackie.

Jackie could sense there was more to the question than the usual perfunctory inquiry. Knowing how quickly the town's talking drums spread news, she knew Kristan would know about Dana's move to Greece. "Fine," Jackie said. "Where's Jennifer?"

"She's —" Kristan stopped.

Jackie saw the tears as Kristan looked away and sensed a detachment that had never been a part of their friendship.

She and Kristan had been friends since grade school. After they had gotten on with their respective careers — Jackie as a doctor and Kristan as a reporter — they had reconnected and had been friends ever since. Their respective partners had been folded into their friendship.

"Jennifer's away."

Jackie thought about what Kristan had said. From the moment her two friends had gotten together, they had been inseparable. "Where's Dana?" Jackie sensed Kristan's need to change the subject.

"New York, business." Jackie paused, unsure how much she wanted to disclose so publicly.

Joni looked from Kristan to Jackie. "You're a reporter here in town, right?" Jackie appreciated Joni's effort to fill the uncomfortable void. Kristan's responses were on autopilot.

"Guilty."

"I've noticed your byline. I like what you write."

"Thanks. That's nice to hear."

"Would you like to join us for dinner?" Jackie asked. "Is that all right with you, Joni?"

"Of course. Please join us."

"Another time." Kristan hesitated, as if faced with a monumental decision. "I'm meeting my editor for dinner tonight."

"Another time then," Jackie said quietly.

"I tried to call you today," Kristan said.

"I got your message, and just as I was about to call you back, we had a minor emergency."

"I understand."

Jackie frowned. Kristan was putting all the words in the right places, but she was not tracking the conversation. "Look, I'm off tomorrow. How about a walk on the beach?" she said to Kristan.

"Sure."

"How about nine o'clock?" Jackie asked

"Sure."

Kristan looked past Jackie into the second dining room. "I see my editor waving at me." She started to walk away and then turned back. "Nice to meet you," she said to Joni.

"Thank you."

Jackie watched as Kristan started to walk away again, then she stopped and turned back to the table. "Jackie, could I just tell you something privately?" She said to Joni, "I don't wish to be rude."

"Please. Stay here, I need to go to the ladies' room, anyway." The two women watched as Joni walked away.

"I have something to tell you." Kristan put her hand on Jackie's shoulder as if she needed the safety of an anchor. "Jennifer has been in Portland for a week. It's a mess."

"I suspected it was something like that. Do you want to talk tonight?"

"No. Let's just go for the walk tomorrow. My brain is on overload. I don't think I could plug another thought into it tonight."

"I'm so sorry. It's about her having a baby."

"No, it's more about me being an ass." Kristan tried to laugh, but the sound seemed to come out more like a choke. "If I talk about this here" — she stopped and swallowed — "I'm going to break down and cry. Look, I'll see you tomorrow. Give my apologies to Joni. She seems like a wonderful lady."

"She is," Jackie said. "I feel so guilty."

"You? Why?"

"Because I should have called you back sooner. I'm sorry, pal. I've been so preoccupied with my own problems that I haven't been available to my friends."

"Same here. Actually, it seems like we both need a walk on the beach tomorrow. I see Joni coming back. I'll see you tomorrow."

"Your friend Kristan seems distracted," Joni said as she sat back down at the table.

"I'd say." Jackie watched Kristan walk away.

"Look," Joni followed her gaze, "would you like to go talk with her? I don't mind waiting."

"No," Jackie's voice was purposeful. "I want to stay right here, but thanks anyway." She picked up her menu and studied it. "Have you ever eaten here?"

"It's been years."

"I would recommend the baked stuffed haddock. It is absolutely delightful." Jackie wanted to rekindle the quiet moment they had shared before they had been interrupted.

The rest of the evening they talked about medical school and the clinic. Jackie liked Joni's sense of humor, and she also found something comforting and compelling about her presence. She was drawn to her quiet and gentle voice; it was as soothing as mint tea on a cold winter morning. Jackie suspected that Joni had a calming effect on everyone.

Although she remained focused on their conversation, Jackie couldn't help but think about Kristan. She had a nagging sense of what was at the root of her friend's pain. But she didn't want to believe that Jennifer's desire to get pregnant, though problematic, could have created this kind of torture. Jackie sighed. What a month, she thought. Her life was falling apart, and now Kristan seemed on the verge of losing it. Jackie forced her mind back to what Joni was saying. Tomorrow, she and Kristan would talk. But for now, tomorrow was a long way away.

Chapter 5

Joni let herself into her house, tossed her keys on the counter, and then stopped to listen to the silence. This was her second year alone, and she still had not gotten used to it. It felt like those times when she had arrived early at the large cathedral in Boston; there was an unsettling quietness that seemed to scream for rustling coats and organ music. She dropped her coat on the chair and looked at the jade plant sitting in the center of the table. "Honey, I'm home," she said to the plant. "Great, now I'm talking to plants," she huffed at herself.

She pulled out the kitchen chair and slipped her flats off. Nurse's shoes were a lot more comfortable, she thought. Better yet, no shoes were a delight, and most of the time she tramped around her house in her bare feet. She liked the feel of the coolness of the floor in winter and the warmth in summer. She missed those long foot rubs after being on her feet all day. Don't go there, she scolded her mind. Don't go there even a little bit. But on nights like tonight, after having been in the company of women, even women with problems, she thought, she missed that closeness.

She'd left Boston soon after Alex had died. She left because she didn't want to hear the sound of familiar voices or see the dolor in their friends' eyes. Two years later, being alone seemed to be a vast uninhabited desert where she was buried in the middle of the sand with just her head sticking out. She could watch life, but not partake of it. She needed to get out more, she decided instantly, maybe join a club. She shook her head. She had never joined a club. First there had been nursing school, and after that she had focused on earning her master's degree. There had never been time to join anything.

She thought about Jackie and smiled as she replayed their evening. It sounded as though Jackie had experienced much the same. First college, then medical school, and finally residency. Never time to focus on things outside of her career. Joni liked the doctor. She liked her amiable personality and the way her patients trusted her. Joni often found herself watching Jackie's hands, silken hands of steel. Her long slender fingers touched more than a patient's health problem; they seemed to reach in and caress the patient's soul. Her voice was soft. Her brown eyes reading beyond the words. She was taller than Joni, and more slender. But it was her sensitivity that resonated with patients and staff alike.

Joni unbuttoned her blouse and thought about the doctor's newfound dilemma and knew it had something to do with the woman who occasionally picked her up at the clinic. She had seen Dana the few times she had had to wait for Jackie, and Joni had felt seduced by her beauty. She could also sense Carin's jealousy. Carin was unequivocally immersed in her own engaging looks, and Joni could discern her resentment whenever Dana was around. Dana made women look at themselves in the mirror and wonder why they had been genetically shortchanged.

Joni smiled; she was glad she didn't have to compete with Dana for Jackie's attention. She saw the look of complete and unrestricted love in Jackie's eyes whenever the woman was near her. But in the last few weeks, she also had sensed a sadness in Jackie. It was clear something was going on in Jackie's life having to do with some kind of change at the clinic. Joni had heard bits and pieces about moving to Greece, but for the most part she had ignored the gossip. She suspected that Dana had a lot to do with it.

She sighed as she slipped on her robe and tied the belt. And now Jackie had an even more immediate problem. She thought about what had happened as they were ready to leave the restaurant. Carin and Darrel had just arrived. The reaction was one of surprise, and then Joni had noted the invidious look in Carin's eyes just seconds before the veneer of sweetened charm took over.

Carin had gushed that she was so happy to see them. Her face was flushed, no doubt from Darrel's having "taken care of her." After the introductions, Carin had asked Jackie if she was doing anything Sunday night. Joni knew where the question was leading, and the minute Jackie said no, Carin had pounced like a rabbit on lettuce.

Joni shook her head. Jackie hadn't had a chance when Carin insisted the doctor have dinner with them. Joni had stood back to watch the exchange and saw the vexed look in Darrel's eyes. He'd tried to give the doctor an out by saying he expected she was too busy, but Carin had insisted, and Jackie couldn't escape.

As an afterthought, Carin had invited her, but Joni had gracefully declined. She knew being home alone was a heap of a lot better than listening to Carin talk about her wonderful life. Joni picked up her dirty clothes and threw them in the hamper. She had thought about warning Jackie about the predatory temperament of the woman, but had rejected the idea, arguing that it wasn't any of her business. And she had to remember that, although she worked for the doctor, she was not her keeper. Although she suspected that if Vera had been there, the doctor wouldn't be facing an evening with Carin and Darrel. Vera, in that efficient office manner she had, would have said that Jackie had an appointment, a phantom appointment, but an appointment.

Chapter 6

Jackie looked at her watch. Nine o'clock. This was a first, Kristan was late. She reached for the telephone, and frowned as Kristan's telephone rang and rang. She bent over and picked up Bob, who was rubbing against her leg. "What should I do, little guy? If I go look for her, she might show up." Jackie scratched Bob behind her ear, and the puppy wiggled her head around to make sure that she didn't miss a spot. "You like that, don't you." Jackie smiled at the big brown eyes. "I don't know a female who doesn't."

She tucked Bob under her arm and went into the kitchen. She set the small ice chest on the chair. She'd already filled it with Poland Springs water and a few sandwiches; she suspected that Kristan had not been eating. She reached in the refrigerator to get some milk for her coffee when she heard the car in the driveway. She set Bob down and opened the door.

"Hi," Kristan said as she got out of the car.

"Hi yourself." Kristan looked tired. Jackie encircled Kristan in her arms and held her tightly against her. How many times over the years had they hugged? This time, they both needed the comfort and security of each other's arms. "I'm glad you're here."

"Me too." Kristan picked up Bob, who was sniffing her feet. "She's grown."

"That's all she does, eat and grow."

"You know I never had a dog as a kid."

"That's too bad. They're a lot of work, but they offer so much in return. They so want to please you."

"Is she going with us?"

"Absolutely. Come on. Let's not waste even a minute of this day." Jackie picked up the cooler.

Kristan reached out her hand to the cooler. "Let me."

"I'm fine."

Kristan dropped her arm. "This is going to be an odd comfort session."

"Why?"

"You're grappling with a move to Greece, and I'm fighting not to lose Jennifer."

"How'd you know about the trip to Greece?"

"Vera. She called me and asked me to talk to you. Little did she know that I was battling my own she-monsters."

"Is it that bad?"

"Yes, no, I don't know." Kristan struggled with words as they walked down to the beach. "I honestly don't know. Jennifer's been gone a week. And when I call her parents, she's either out or in bed."

"Avoidance is not Jennifer's style."

"No, but it is now."

"What happened?" Jackie picked Bob up and lifted her

over a large rock. The puppy's feet slipped on the gravel, and Jackie reached under her butt to steady her climb.

Kristan kept walking, heedless of Jackie's efforts to help her pup. "You want to sit here?" Kristan gestured at a cluster of boulders.

"Sure." Jackie set the ice cooler on the rock next to her and sat down. She handed Kristan a Poland Springs and a sandwich. "What happened?" she repeated.

"Well," Kristan stopped. "When I got home the night she'd been at your office, there was candlelight and lobsters. Bette Midler's "The Rose" was playing in the background. I thought I'd forgotten an anniversary or something." Kristan drew a finger over her lips. "She kissed me and I was on fire. We've been together twelve years, and that woman's kiss could thaw a glacier. We had this romantic dinner, and I kept asking her what I'd forgotten. She'd just smile and say it was a surprise. By the end of dinner, I was fired up with curiosity and desire, and that's when she told me about her visit to your office. God" — Kristan smacked the palm of her hand against her forehead — "Jacks, she read something in my face. Surprise, doubt, I don't know, whatever, all I know is I was stunned."

"But why? Jennifer told me you'd talked about having a child all the time."

Kristan set her uneaten sandwich down next to her and gnawed on her bottom lip. "She'd talk, I'd agree." Kristan wiped her tears with the edge of her sweatshirt. "But I wasn't ready for an actuality test. This sounds like such an excuse, but I thought we had it all. Great careers, each other. I thought that was enough. But I was wrong. I hurt her deeply. She had wanted excitement and support from me, and all I gave her was an unintelligible facial expression. But she knew, Jacks, she knew I was not prepared for that kind of commitment."

"What happened?"

Kristan inhaled a sob. "She blew out the candles and just walked away, both physically and mentally. She worked the rest of that week, told me that she had asked for a leave of absence at the DA's office, and she . . . was . . . gone," Kristan dragged out the words.

"I don't understand. Didn't you tell her what was going on in your head?"

"I tried. I told her I was feeling all this jealousy. I didn't want to share her even with a child. I didn't want the complications in our life."

Jackie groaned. "I feel partial responsibility for this."

Kristan looked at Jackie. "You? Why?"

"I wished I could have called you at the office, warned you. But it would have been a breach of patient confidentiality. I'm sorry."

"I'm not going to let you take even a second of responsibility for this. It was me, Jacks, my stupid, childish jealousy. Afterwards, I tried to explain my reaction, but she just kept turning inward. This wasn't a simple fight over what color sheets to put on the bed, this was . . . this was cosmic pain. I've really hurt her. The night she told me she was going to her parent's house, I begged . . ." Kristan's voice broke. "I begged, pleaded with her to stay."

Jackie reached over and stroked Bob's neck. Bob was trying to grub under a rock with her nose.

"You know why she left." It was a statement not a question.

Jackie nodded. "I suspect. Jennifer felt she offered you the most perfect gift and you disappointed her."

"I figured that out but much later. I told her I wanted a child, our child, but my words never stretched far enough to reach her. They just died in the air."

"Do you want a child?"

"Now, yes."

"Because you really want a baby, or because you want Jennifer back?"

"In those revealing moments we have late at night when it's just us stuck in the solitude of our minds, I don't. And I

49

know why. I'm selfish. I don't want life to change. Jennifer used to call what we had our Aphrodite bond; I was terrified of losing that. But as paralyzed as I am in that maelstrom of doubt" — Kristan stopped tossing tiny rocks in the water and looked at Jackie — "I forgot the most important thing. I broke a covenant, and that is why Jennifer left. Now, sitting here talking with you, yeah, I want a child. I just hope it's not too late to convince Jennifer."

"Because you want Jennifer back or because you truly want a child?" Jackie repeated. "You realize, Kristan, that indecision is a cancer cluster, it devours everything in its path. Jennifer will know."

"I realized that this morning when I was driving to your house. And that is as brutally honest as it gets."

"Kristan, we've known each other since grade school. What I don't understand is why you're sitting here. Why aren't you in Portland telling this to Jennifer?"

"The day she left I called, but her mother told me Jennifer needed time and space to think this through."

"I don't agree. Time and space will grow into an unlimited distance, something that can't be fixed or reached."

"But what if she refuses to see me?"

"Jennifer's wounded, but this isn't the time for you two to be apart. You need to be resolving this together."

They shared a small silence as Jackie watched Kristan struggle with the idea.

"What if . . ." Kristan stopped. "What if she says it's over? I can't handle that," Jackie could hear the worry in Kristan's voice.

"I don't know," Jackie said cautiously. "I want to say don't worry, but that's ridiculous. I hate it when people tell me not to worry, when what I want to do is worry. That's why you have to confront this. But I'd say you should be prepared for the worst possible answer."

Kristan shook her head. "That's not what I wanted to

hear. I wanted you to say that Jennifer has the capacity to forgive. That's what I wanted to hear."

"*Forgive* may be the wrong word. I think you need to start with trying to get Jennifer to understand, and then maybe she can work on forgiveness."

"You know what's funny? Not funny ha-ha, but strange? At one time I believed there wasn't a thing in the universe that could separate us." Kristan shrugged. "I never worried about another woman because Jennifer is single-minded in her commitments." Bewildered, Kristan tugged at stands of her hair. "God, I feel like I woke up one morning to find that I'd been sucked into a huge wave and that I'm ricocheting off it like a storm-tossed ship," Kristan sighed. "But you're right. My being here is just me afraid to confront the worst. I'll go," Kristan said quietly. "Look," she pointed at Bob.

Jackie looked to where Kristan was pointing and laughed as she watched her puppy try to bite at the waves.

"I'll go today. Thank you, my friend. But what about you? Are you going to Greece?"

"I don't think so, I don't know, I . . ." Jackie stopped. "I want to say no, but then I think, well . . . maybe." Jackie said the words again as if trying them on for a second time. "Dana won't understand this indecisiveness."

"Have you talked about this with her?"

"I've tried, but I'm scared." Jackie felt relief. Finally she had said the word out loud.

"Scared of change?"

Jackie frowned. "Yes, and of leaving here and uprooting my life and . . . and . . . and . . . Now we live in two worlds, but we're together for about six of twelve months. When she moves to Greece, who knows how much time she would have to come back here? Probably two weeks at the most. I would become her vacation." Frustrated Jackie picked up a pebble and threw it at the water. The movement distracted Bob from playing with the waves and she ran toward her. "We can't be together if I stay here. And we both know that. So I'm the one who has to make the commitment to change my life."

Bob ran up to Jackie and licked her hand. Jackie reached out to touch her head and felt her shiver. Jackie smoothed a spot on her sweatshirt and placed the wet pup against her stomach and folded the bottom of her sweatshirt against the black-and-white fur. Bob rested her wet nose against Jackie's hand. With her other hand, she stroked Bob's head.

"When Dana's here she fills my nights with ecstasy and my days with joy. But in those critical moments when you're really at one with your mind, I know that I want feather-bed comfort here in Bailey's Cove and that she wants purple-and-fine-linen excitement in that world out there. She'd never be content living here, and I know I'd never be happy living anywhere else." Jackie leaned back on her elbows.

"Why not just go on with what you have?"

"Because it's not making either of us happy." Jackie reached inside the cooler, twisted the cap off a second bottle of water, and drank deeply. She blotted her lips against the back of her hand. Bob whimpered when the hand moved away from her head. "Funny, a few weeks ago, I thought I was happy. But it's so different."

"You don't want to go back to being alone?"

"Kristan, I am alone. That's what I figured out in the last few days. When some monumental thing happens in our lives, our connection is with Ma Bell. We can't hug and jump up and down and whoop. I love Dana; she's the only woman since Marianne died who reached inside my soul and built a fire. But when she's gone, I'm alone."

"What does Dana want?"

"Me, in Greece." Jackie rubbed Bob's ear between her two fingers. Bob opened one eye, then closed it again and settled into another puppy nap.

Kristan said, "May I be permitted to offer an observation, one you're not going to like?"

"Of course. But don't be surprised if it makes me angry. A lot of things make me angry of late."

Kristan sucked in her breath. "This trip isn't going to break you two up because you've never been together. You're weekend lovers who happen to love each other. But you're not a family," Kristan stopped. "Don't get me wrong. Jennifer and I adore Dana. But she's a tidal wave crashing down on the beach; but when the water retreats, all that's left is an empty beach filled with the flotsam and jetsam of the moments you've shared. That's been your relationship from the beginning, and it's not going to change. What happens after three years in Greece? She'll want to go back to freelancing, because that's what gives her work its bold and timeless beauty. For her the challenge is seeing things through the lens of her camera." Kristan paused. "Neither of you are really happy except when you're working. That's the one constancy of your lives. Not each other, but each one's profession." Kristan stopped.

"I want to be angry at you," Jackie said quietly, not looking at Kristan. "But it would be an empty anger because you're right. Last night, Joni suggested that the most we can expect in life when we get older is fifty percent of happiness, but I don't agree with her. I don't think fifty percent can sustain you. There has to be more, otherwise why bother?"

Kristan leaned her head against her knee. "Look at us, a couple of aging lesbians. We're supposed to have this combined wisdom and all we have is, what? Brains that are starting to shred and fractured hearts. Hell of a senior moment."

Jackie laughed. "I can't argue with that. You're the lady who paints pictures with words."

"In my muddled mind last night, I got the impression that Joni is one neat lady."

"I like her." Jackie thought about how relaxed they had been with one another. Like old friends. Then her mind jumped to the end of the evening and Carin's invitation. She had said yes to the dinner invitation before she realized, and now she was hoping a medical emergency would rescue her. "She has only been at the clinic a few weeks, but I feel a symbiotic working relationship with her."

"She reminds me of Marianne," Kristan said. "That soft voice and those brown eyes that seems to absorb everything. Last night she knew something was wrong with me and she quickly tried to ameliorate the situation with conversation. Marianne would have done that."

"Marianne?" Jackie stared at the waves. She felt a calm settle over her as she synchronized her thoughts with their rhythm. She nodded her head. "Maybe."

"I could be wrong." Kristan ran both hands through her hair. "My sensitivity plane has been rather tilted of late, but maybe what we're both sensing is that she's gay. That remote detection that goes off when we discern one of our own."

Jackie scowled at her friend. "I don't know. Besides, that question is not on the job application. Nor was it on her résumé. It doesn't matter. She is good. Remember that emergency I mentioned to you last night? It was as if we'd worked together forever. I didn't have to ask her to pass this or that. She anticipated my every move. It was nice." Exhausted from thinking about herself, she turned the conversation back to Kristan. "But what about you, my tormented friend?"

"I'm going to do just what the doctor ordered. I'm going to Portland today, now, this moment," Kristan said as she stood up. "I don't want to lose another minute of life without Jennifer. I can make this work. But" — Kristan brushed the gravel from her hands — "I have to say one thing, though, about Dana. As painful as this indecision is that you're going through, I'm glad she came into your life." She reached out a hand and pulled Jackie to a standing position.

"Why?" Bob lifted her head from the warm nest Jackie had built against her stomach, and Jackie set her down on the rocks. Bob yawned then jumped up and scampered off toward the water.

"After Marianne died you withdrew and your friends were worried. You went through the motions of life. You'd go to work and go home. You were living, but you didn't have a life. Does that make sense?"

"Yes, it does. Dana really wants those three years in Greece, and I really want them for her. I just don't know if I want to be there also. Vera says I'd be miserable if I left."

"I suspect Vera is right. Any chance she might give it up?"

"No, she signed the contract not knowing if I would join her or not. It was her way of making the decision. And that makes me angry." Jackie felt like she wanted to kick a rock. "She didn't want to talk it over first. I feel like I've lost some kind of race."

"Not a race," Kristan said delicately. "But look at it from her perspective. If she had waited to talk it over with you, there would have been hours of discussion about your going or not, about her going or not. Maybe she was scared you'd talk her out of it. Maybe that's what she was afraid of."

"Maybe." Jackie felt the tears and turned away.

"Jackie, you're my dearest friend." Jackie could hear Kristan's hesitancy.

"Say it." She choked.

"I think you two have been breaking up from the beginning. Remember your words? You're weekend lovers."

Jackie put her head in her hands and sobbed.

"Come here. We both need a good cry." Kristan held out her arms. "You know I figured that your deceptively composed demeanor was just that. I know you well, and you're grieving already."

"Yes," Jackie sobbed.

"When does she get back?"

Jackie stepped back and wiped her tears on her sleeve. "Monday night."

"When does she leave for Greece?"

"A few weeks."

"Not much time."

"No. I could delay my leaving if I decided to go. I haven't even told the board at the clinic that I am thinking about leaving. That would buy me a few months. Get a doctor in to replace me."

"That only buys you more pain." Kristan looked deep into Jackie's eyes. "Don't do that. Make the decision now."

Jackie closed her eyes. "I know," she said quietly. "I know that I don't want to go."

"Tell her."

"I'll try." Jackie felt as though a battle were raging inside her head. She put a palm against her forehead and wished she could push the warring thoughts away. She bent over, tossed the half-eaten sandwiches into the cooler, and put the top on. In her other hand, she picked up Bob, who had curled up next to a rock.

Kristan reached for the cooler. "Let me." The two walked silently up the path.

When they reached Kristan's car, Jackie stopped. "Kristan, let's talk about your problem." She looked deep into her friend's eyes. "Do me one favor. Let's both be prepared for the worst."

"I know and hope for the best." She smiled over her cynicism.

"Don't hope for the best," Jackie interrupted. "I saw Jennifer's excitement when she was at the clinic. This may be a Humpty Dumpty theme unfolding."

"Humpty Dumpty." Kristan reached over and stroked Bob's head. "Oh, I get it. The dumb egg that fell off the wall."

"Mostly the ending. You can't put Humpty Dumpty back together again."

"I'll . . ." Kristan cleared her throat. "I'll prepare for the worst. But if I don't hope for the best, Jacks, I won't be able to put one foot in front of the other. What about you?"

"Today I'm resolved that this is going to end right for both of us. But tonight when I'm alone I'll think differently."

"I know." Kristan sighed. "That's why I'm leaving for Portland now. Because if I think about it, I'll question the wisdom of it. Right now it seems right, and I'm just going to do it and not think about it." Kristan handed the cooler to Jackie. "I'm drowning and Jennifer is my life preserver. I've got to do it."

"I know. I just want you to be prepared for the worst possible scenario. Anything after that will seem like a gift."

Kristan opened the car door. "You're right. We both need to be prepared. Be gentle with yourself, my friend."

"You too." Jackie hugged Kristan before she got into her car.

"You know what I hope? I hope that this will all go away and that we can both get back to what we had," Kristan said through her car window.

"Me too." Jackie closed Kristan's door and watched as she started it up. Kristan waved to her one last time before she turned onto the road. "Me too." Jackie said to the air.

Chapter 7

Jackie woke up Sunday ill prepared for what lay ahead. Saturday night she and Dana had talked, each dancing on the edge of what was really on their minds. Dana would be back in Bailey's Cove Monday night, and Jackie wanted to stay focused on what she and her lover had to talk about. She didn't feel in a social mood, let alone like having dinner with her nurse and her husband. But she didn't know how to get out of it. She'd never been good at cocktail chitchat. Those few times she had been forced to do it during medical school or while in residency, Marianne had always been there and everything seemed to turn out right somehow.

Sunday morning, she'd called Joni in hopes that she could convince her to join her at Carin's house, but she got her answering machine. She didn't leave a message. Oh well, she thought, if nothing else they could always talk about the clinic. She'd tell Carin about her plans of adding another doctor and one or two more nurses.

Sunday afternoon she finished her rounds and followed the map Carin had given her at the restaurant. She followed Route 1 toward Bayport and then turned left on Route 190. She was to follow a dirt road about two miles and then look for a mailbox with a picture of a plumber on it.

Jackie stopped and backed her car up when she saw the mailbox. She pulled down a long driveway and noted the small white cape just to her right. Jackie reached for the bottle of wine and saw Carin walking toward the car.

"Dr. Claymont, I'm just so pleased you could join us. Darrel said he couldn't be happier." Carin reached for the bottle. "For us? Well, thank you. You didn't have to bring a thing." Carin slipped her arm through Jackie's and walked with her to the door. "Did you have a busy afternoon?"

"So, so. I had to make rounds —"

"Darrel, just look who's here."

"Hey, Doc," Darrel called from the living room.

"I can't tear that man away from baseball. He's just glued to the set. Come in, sit down. We're just dying to get to know you. Would you like something to drink? I've got beer, wine, whatever."

Jackie noticed the beer cans sitting next to Darrel's lounge chair. "A glass of wine would be fine."

"Good. Now, Darrel, you visit with Dr. Claymont while I'm in the kitchen."

"Who you pulling for?" Jackie asked by way of conversation.

"Boston, but they're losing. They always lose," Darrel took a deep drink of his beer. "You like baseball?"

"Haven't watched it in years." Jackie turned back to the screen. "I see what you mean," she said looking at the small scoreboard the network flashed in the corner of the screen.

The scoreboard seemed almost minuscule when compared with the huge fifty-six inch, big-screen television set that the players were running around on. She had never seen a television that large except in the store at Sears. She'd often wondered what kind of people would buy such a monstrosity. Now she knew.

Carin breezed into the room and handed Jackie her drink. "We've just been so excited that you were coming today. Why, you're our first company. 'Cept for Darrel's family."

"Chase? You must be related to Darren Chase. I set his arm several years ago."

"He's my brother."

"They're a real close family. I just love that. I have family back in Atlanta. I'm hoping to get Momma and Daddy to visit us this summer. They never have been out of Atlanta. Daddy says he'd die up here, 'cause it's too cold. If they come up, I want them to meet you. I told them all about you and what a nice little clinic I was working in. 'Course when I was in Atlanta, I worked in big hospitals. I told Momma and Daddy this was more fun 'cause you got a real chance to know the patients."

"Yes, that is a nice part of working in a small town." Jackie wondered who was more ill at ease, her or Carin.

Carin prattled on. "We're eating early 'cause Darrel has to be in Houlton at six in the morning. So he's going to watch the rest of the game and go to bed. That's a three-hour drive for him. Isn't it sugar? Why I just forgot when I invited you on Friday night that he had to get up early. 'Course Darrel says he wants me to invite guests, gives me a chance to make new friends. Isn't that right, sugar?"

"Yup."

"I tell you what," Carin said. "You just sit here with Darrel one more minute. I'll fix him a plate, and then you and I can go to the kitchen for a nice visit."

Jackie watched Carin as she rushed out of the room. She sneaked a peek at her watch. Only ten minutes had gone by. She leaned back against the couch and sipped her wine. Carin returned carrying a large tray heaped full of potatoes and what looked like roast beef. She set the tray on Darrel's lap and unfolded the napkin for him. "Here ya go, babe. You need anything, just holler. Come on, Dr. Claymont, I have dinner set up for us in the kitchen."

Jackie started to say something to Darrel but changed her mind. His right hand was shoveling food in his mouth as his left pushed up the sound on the remote.

"Well, isn't this nice," Carin said once they were seated at the table. "I've been meaning to invite you over for dinner since we first met, but just didn't have a chance."

"That's very nice of you," Jackie looked at all the food on the table. Besides the roast beef and potatoes, there were three kinds of vegetables, rolls, a gelatin salad, and coleslaw. "My, it looks as though you've been cooking all day."

"I love to cook," Carin said as she handed Jackie the potatoes. "I learned to cook early on. My momma was a sewer and worked in a factory in Atlanta, so as soon as we girls were old enough we were put to work in the kitchen. Daddy worked on the railroad and he demanded his supper be on the table by five o'clock every day. Never could change the menu either. It was meat and potatoes every day."

"So what made you decide to become a nurse?"

"I used to love to watch *Marcus Welby* on television, and I just adored his nurse. I'd watch it every week without fail. Told Momma that's what I wanted to be. She said she wanted me to be anything but a sewer. It was awful hard work. Once I graduated from high school, I had to convince Daddy to let me go to nursing school. I got in and, well, here we are," she said as she handed Jackie more food.

"What made you decide to come up here?"

"Darrel wanted to start his own plumbing and heating business. You ever need anything done at your house, you let me know. Darrel's the best."

"That's good to know," Jackie said as she tasted the roast beef. "My, this is delicious."

"It's my grandmomma's recipe. Big family secret," Carin beamed. "So what made you decide to become a doctor? Did you used to watch *Marcus Welby?*"

"No, actually it's something I'd wanted to do from the time I could remember. My parents encouraged me first to attend college and then medical school. I was fortunate to return here and set up the clinic after a few years of private practice. Actually, Vera and I set up the clinic."

"Yes, I know. She's such a doll. I just love her to death. She's so efficient, keeps that office humming like a new machine."

For the next hour they talked. Or as Jackie thought about it later, Carin talked about herself, Darrel, and her family and Jackie listened. Carin seemed to punctuate each chapter of her life by pouring more wine into her glass. Jackie slowly sipped the wine she had been given with dinner.

Looking at Jackie's glass, Carin said, "Drink up, Doctor. I have more in the refrigerator."

"No more for me, thanks. I have to stop by the hospital."

"I got to tell you" — Carin set the wine bottle next to her plate — "I was just fascinated by that lovely woman friend of yours. Vera tells me that's her niece. And what a lovely niece she has and what an exciting career."

"Yes, Dana is fortunate. She gets to see the world through the eye of a camera."

"You been friends long?"

"We grew up together, although she was several years younger than me. What about you? How'd you and Darrel meet?" Jackie said as she changed the subject. She decided that given the amount of wine Carin had had, she probably didn't remember that she'd already told Jackie the story.

Jackie listened as Carin talked on and on about Darrel for the next thirty minutes. Both women looked up as Darrel carried his tray into the kitchen.

"Game over?" Carin purred.

"Yeah. Boston lost again. Look, sorry to be rude, Doc, but I have to hit the sack now. Got to get up before the chickens."

Jackie stood up and shook Darrel's hand. "It was very nice meeting you, again."

"Same here." Darrel leaned down and gave his wife a passionate kiss on the mouth. Jackie looked away. "See ya later, babe."

"Let me help with dishes," Jackie offered.

"Don't be silly. I have all the pots and pans washed, and these few dishes can wait until later. Let's go in the living room and visit."

Seated on the couch, Jackie looked around. The television was on but muted. There were pictures of Carin and Darrel and pictures of what probably were her momma and daddy. Jackie glanced at her watch.

"Well, isn't this nice." Carin sat on the couch next to Jackie.

"So you were telling me about how you and Darrel met."

"We met in a bar in Atlanta." Jackie noted that Carin had a sparkle in her eyes that Jackie suspected was caused more by the wine than the excitement of recounting her life with Darrel. Carin talked on about their meeting and how long they dated. All the romantic places they went to on their honeymoon and finally their move to Bailey's Cove. "So what about you? I'm just fascinated about your friend Dana's career. Tell me some of the places she's been."

"She's been all over Europe and most of Africa. She's traveled to some South American countries, but she mostly concentrates her shoots in Europe."

"What's her favorite place?"

"Bailey's Cove."

"You're kidding. Bailey's Cove. She's been to such

63

romantic places as Italy and France, and her favorite place is right here? That's hard to believe."

"This is home. Don't you think there's always a special place in your heart for where you were born?"

"Well, maybe." Carin sounded doubtful. "Does she have a house here?"

"No, she stays with me when she's between shoots."

"Well, isn't that nice of you. I'd love to have a friend like that. 'Course Darrel wouldn't want me to get too chummy with anyone. He's the jealous type. He likes me right here."

"Darrel is right." Jackie looked down at her watch for the fifth time that evening. "Wow, look at the time. I've got to stop at the hospital before I head for home."

"Oh, do you have to go so soon?" Carin touched Jackie's arm, her fingers lingering there.

"Yes." Jackie stood up and put her hands in her pocket. "I have some patients I visit more than once on Sundays. I call it 'social medicine.' They're folks alone, and a friendly face helps, even if it's only their doctor's friendly face."

Carin stood very close to Jackie. "Well, I'm so glad you could visit," she said, walking her to the door. "Down south we give our new friends a hug," she said as she slipped her arms around Jackie's neck.

Jackie was startled at the intimacy of the hug. She stepped back and bumped up against the door. "Thank you for dinner."

"Well, we'll do this again, I promise. Maybe you could invite your friend Dana."

"I'll see you at the clinic tomorrow," Jackie said. "Again, thanks for dinner."

"You're welcome. Let me walk you to your car."

"Really, that won't be necessary." Jackie closed the door behind her and went directly to her car. She slipped it into gear and drove down the driveway. Strange, she thought. Really strange.

Chapter 8

Joni pulled into the driveway at the hospital, threw a jacket over her sweats, and went inside. She stopped at the reception desk. "Could you tell me what room Ceila Wheaton is in?"

"Room two-twenty-four," the receptionist answered without looking up.

"Thank you." Joni followed the signs to Room 224. "Hey, Auntie," she said as soon as she entered.

"Well, sweetie, so nice of you to visit. How'd you find out I was here?"

Joni leaned over and gave her aunt a kiss on the cheek. "Your daughter called me, asked me to look in on you."

"That girl. I told her not to bother you."

"She's worried, Auntie. Guess you gave her and Roger a real scare."

"Twaddle. I just had a few chest pains. Made Roger run me to the hospital. Messed up my Sunday night television. Can't find anything I like on this set," she said as her thumb worked the remote, forcing the channels to race up and down. "They don't even have HBO. What kind of place doesn't have HBO?"

Joni laughed and sat down. "A hospital. You're here for tests, not television. So tell me about the pains."

"'Twern't nothing. I was playing with my grandchildren in the backyard, when all of a sudden I felt a shortness of breath and these pains." Joni watched as her aunt's free hand went to her chest. "Felt like a small horse sitting on my chest. Sarah got scared and screamed for Roger. He came running, and as fast as you could crack a clam he had me in the car. I bet he drove ninety miles an hour to get here. Liked to scare the wind right out of me. In the emergency room they poked and probed, then said they were putting me in the hospital. I told them I was fine and wanted to go home. They said I couldn't and Roger agreed with them. Can they keep me here like that?"

"They sure can, especially after I talk to the doctor and tell him not to let you out until you're better."

"You wouldn't."

"I would. Sarah told me your family doctor is Dr. Larson. As soon as I leave here, I plan to call him."

"You're just as bad as Sarah. All a stew about nothing."

Joni suppressed a smile.

"So what happens to me next?" Joni could read the worry in her aunt's eyes.

"They'll run some tests, see if there's any blockage."

"Well, they're not going to cut on me. I plan on leaving this world with the parts God issued me."

"I doubt they'll remove any parts." Joni's smile was impish. "But they may do a little tinkering."

"Well, they ain't tinkering. I'm seventy-eight years old and had a good life —"

"That's not too old for tinkering," Joni interrupted.

"You're just trying to get a rise out of me. You're contrary like your mother, God rest her soul. She used to do that to me all the time when we were growing up." Her aunt shook a finger at her. "You've got your mother's temperament, Joni Coan. You can't fool me."

"I'm not trying to fool you —"

"I thought I recognized that voice." Both women looked up as Jackie walked into the room.

"What are you doing here?" Jackie and Joni asked each other at the same time.

"You go first," Jackie said with a chuckle.

"This is my Aunt Ceila Wheaton, she decided to interrupt my Sunday night by faking some chest pains. Auntie, this is my boss, Dr. Jackie Claymont."

"Pleased to meet you." Ceila held out her hand to the doctor. "And I wasn't faking. Don't listen to this girl. She just likes to get a rise out of me. Joni tells me you're the next best thing to growing hair."

Jackie laughed. "I don't know about that."

"What are you doing here? I thought you were having dinner with Carin." Joni suppressed an urge to drag out the woman's name.

"Yes, well, it was a rather early dinner. Seems Darrel had to be up at three to go to a job in Houlton, so I thought it best to leave early." Jackie looked up at the clock. She'd left Carin's at seven and had hotfooted it to the hospital. Jackie noted the amused look on Joni's face. "I called to invite you along, but alas your answering machine did most of the talking for you today."

"I'm sorry. I've been in Cutler all day. I was hiking. When I got home . . ." Joni frowned. "There weren't any messages from you. Just one from my cousin Sarah asking me to check on my aunt."

"I didn't leave any. I figured if you were out, there wasn't any point in leaving one, but you missed a really great pot roast dinner, with potatoes and corn and peas and broccoli and rolls and —"

"Whoa, you're making me put on inches just thinking about all that food."

"Come to think of it," Ceila interrupted, "I didn't get my dinner. Roger whisked me off so fast, I didn't get a thing to eat. You figure you can find me the fixin's for a sandwich?" she asked her niece.

"The cafeteria is still open, but I don't know what kind of diet the doctor might put you on. Her physician is Dr. Larson," she told Jackie.

"Know him well; he's a good doctor."

"Yes he is, and he knows better than to put me on a diet. I've been eating this way for seventy-eight years and I ain't changing. Now, I'd like a turkey sandwich on white with lettuce and tomato. I'd like a dill pickle and a nice cup of coffee."

Joni looked helplessly at Jackie. "Can she eat that?"

"What's Dr. Larson say?"

"I plan to call him when I leave here."

"You don't have to. I'm here," came a voice from the corridor. "Nice to see you, Jackie," he shook her hand.

"John." Jackie smiled affectionately at the older man. She'd known him a long time and, although his practice was in Bayport, they often saw each other at the hospital.

"And Joni," he held out his arms to hug her. "Sarah told me she'd gotten ahold of you. Welcome back."

"Thank you." Joni returned the hug.

"Well, Ceila, what ya been up to?" Dr. Larson was reading her chart.

"There's nothing in there I can't tell you," she retorted. She then told him about her chest pains and shortness of breath. "But right now I'm starving, and this niece of mine won't get me a turkey sandwich."

"Go ahead. I want to examine your aunt," he said to Joni. "Would you like to stay, Jackie?"

"No, you go ahead. I think I'll help Joni in her quest for a turkey sandwich on white with lettuce and tomato."

"Good girl." Ceila beamed at the doctor.

Outside her aunt's room Joni whispered, "You don't have to do this. I know you're busy."

"I wouldn't miss this for the world. Your realize our small cafeteria might be serving chicken or liver and not turkey."

"I got that covered," Joni smiled up at the doctor. "I'm going to the sandwich shop."

"Let's take my car," Jackie said.

Joni recounted her day of hiking and listened attentively as Jackie related her early evening at the Chases'. "She hugged you?" Joni repeated.

"Yeah, it was the strangest thing. Very awkward and forced. I've been thinking about it since it happened, and I sure as heck can't figure it out," Jackie said as she turned into the parking lot of the sandwich shop.

"Look, I have to spend another thirty minutes with my aunt, would you like to get a cup of coffee or something?"

"I'd love to." Jackie felt relieved. She had felt unnerved after leaving Carin's. She had driven by Kristan's house, but her car was gone. Jackie understood her determination and her need to leave for Portland immediately on Saturday. "Do you mind having a cup at my house? Bob's been inside for a couple of hours, and I'm feeling guilty."

"Bob?"

"My dog."

"I'd love to. Would you like a sandwich or something?"

"No, thanks. I feel like I'll never eat again. You can't imagine how much food that woman had on her table."

While Jackie waited for Joni to get the sandwich, she scanned one of her medical journals. Their trip back to the hospital was a comfortable silence.

"I'll see you at the house, say around eight? I'll be finished with my patients in another fifteen minutes. You know where I live?"

"The large captain's house, with the widow's walk and the best view of Bailey's Cove."

"Some would argue one of the better views, but yeah, I'm kinda partial to it." They were in the entryway of the hospital. "See you then."

Chapter 9

Jackie put on a fresh pot of coffee and then fed Bob. She'd stood outside and watched as the pup scampered around the backyard looking for that perfect place to piddle. It always amazed her how hard dogs worked a backyard in search of that perfect blade of grass. A dog expert had said it was their way of picking up their mail. She looked up when she heard Joni's car. "I have a fresh pot brewing, and I stopped at the store and picked up some doughnuts."

"Thank you, and this must be Bob." Joni reached down to stroke the puppy's head and then followed Jackie inside. "I love what you've done with this kitchen. I was in the house a few times when the Archers owned it. I remember Mable had something blocking every window, but this is wonderful," Joni said as she stared out the sliding glass doors. The full moon was just coming up over the bay, and the light dancing on the tiny ripples in the water looked like a million flickering candles.

"I remember that," Jackie said as she set Bob down. "The first time I had a tour of the house, I walked into the kitchen and she had glass shelves in front of every window, and the shelves were full of plants. You had to peek between leaves and vines to see even a sliver of the bay. After I bought the house, I took down all the shelves and had carpenters knock out every wall that faced the ocean and add sliding glass doors. I wanted to see the water."

"It's beautiful. And Bob is adorable." She reached down to stroke the pup's ear. Bob licked her fingers.

"Thank you. She rules. So don't be surprised if she tries to show off in front of you. How about a cup of coffee?"

"I'd love it. Okay if I hold her? I haven't been around a pup in a long time."

"Sure, she loves the attention."

Joni watched as Jackie poured two cups of coffee.

"How do you take yours?"

"Like my tea, straight up."

Jackie picked up the two cups. "Follow me. So how's your aunt doing?" Jackie set the cups on the coffee table and motioned for Joni to sit down.

"Fine. Dr. Larson seems to think she hasn't suffered any permanent heart damage. He plans to keep her in for a few days and run some tests. She was just squealing when I left. Threatened to walk out. I told her that if she did she'd walk out in her hospital gown because I was going to hide all her clothes. Actually," Joni sipped her coffee. "I think for all her protestations, she's relieved. My cousin Sarah had just gotten there when I was about to leave, so she was fine. I'm going to stop by and visit her tomorrow. What about you? Sounds like you had quite an evening."

"Different is the way I've been assessing it. I've been

thinking about it since I left, and I think I'm overreacting. Although . . ." Jackie paused and absently traced a circle around the lip of her cup. "I thought she seemed rather nervous." She took a sip. "But then I got to thinking, Southerners tend to be more touchy-feely than us New Englanders. I figure she's lonely and just looking for a good friend. I feel sorry for her. Although Darrel seems nice enough, he was focused on baseball and couldn't have cared less if we were there or not."

"What exactly happened?"

Jackie related the story of her arrival and abbreviated conversation with Darrel and her conversation with Carin. "Anyway, she seemed nervous. Her mouth ran like a jackhammer. When I got up to leave she put her arms around my neck and hugged me. I wasn't sure what to do, because I've never been hugged by one of my nurses before. So I sort of put my hands on her shoulders and gave her a quick pat and then stepped back. Actually, I banged into the door." She laughed. "After that, I left. It was really awkward, and I must admit I felt uncomfortable. Don't get me wrong, I hug my friends. It just seemed strange. I guess that's the only way I can describe it."

"Did she say anything?"

"Just that she was happy I could come over and said she wanted to do it again. Then I left and went straight to the hospital. Anyway, I'm sure I'm overreacting. Like I said, I think she's lonely."

"Probably," Joni said thoughtfully. "I understand she's only been up here a few months, and it seems from what she's told me that Darrel's family isn't really crazy about her."

"Really, that's too bad. Has she said why?"

"Yes and no. She seems to think they're upset because he married a girl from the South instead of one of the locals. But I find that hard to believe. Geography seems like a strange reason to dislike someone." Joni stroked Bob's neck. The puppy had collapsed between them on the couch.

73

"Anyway, that was a strange couple of hours. Like I said, I'm probably reading too much into it. The next few days are going to be difficult," Jackie said, more to convince herself.

"I'm sorry," Joni stopped stroking the puppy's neck and looked intently at Jackie. "Do you want to talk about it?"

Jackie hesitated.

"Look, I'm sorry. I seem to blunder into these difficult areas. It's really none of my business."

"It's no secret . . ." Jackie rested her chin on the back of her hand. "That Dana and I are lovers. I hope that doesn't offend you," Jackie stared into Joni's eyes, trying to read her reaction.

"Hardly." Joni laughed. "Were you worried that I was going to have some kind of homophobic attack and run screaming from the room?"

"No," Jackie laughed, diffusing some of her anxiety. "Actually, I wasn't. Anyway, between Dana's career and my practice we spend abbreviated months together, with me here and her off to some very exciting areas. She's a photojournalist."

"Vera said. It sounds intriguing." Joni nodded at the picture that was sitting on the table next to Jackie's arm. "She's more beautiful in person. Actually, more gorgeous in person. I can see why Carin reacted."

"She is. But I don't understand. What do you mean when you say, why Carin reacted?"

"It was all she talked about after she'd met her," Joni paused. "Some women. No, some *people* just react differently to beautiful people. I think Carin compares herself with Dana, sees her as a rival in some strange kind of way. Wants everyone to think she's just as beautiful. I can't explain it . . . Just something I sense."

"And you, do you see Dana as some kind of rival?" Jackie frowned.

"I don't know. Probably. I think a lot of us subconsciously compare ourselves to someone as beautiful as Dana. I guess it's just all part of our insecurities. I'm not saying I've sat and sulked about it like Carin, but I think it's natural to compare. But I have a feeling that what you're struggling with has something to do with Dana. And I just hate to see the pain that is so evident in your eyes." Joni stopped. "I'm sorry, I shouldn't have said that. Really, it's none of my business."

"Why? For telling me the truth. You're right." Jackie sipped her coffee. "Dana has accepted an assignment in Greece. She wants me to join her."

"And you? Do you want to go to Greece?"

"I don't know. Dana loves her job." Jackie scratched the back of her head. "And I'm happy for her because I don't know how many people I've treated for stress and stress-related diseases because they hate their jobs. But what has complicated this three-month formula is a new job offer. Dana has signed a contract with a prestigious magazine company in Greece. She's agreed to do all of their photo artwork. It's a wonderful opportunity, and she gets to stay in one country. Into this formula she has factored my leaving the clinic and joining her there. A three-year leave of absence, actually."

"Wow. Your patients are going to be disappointed. How soon is this supposed to happen?"

"She's in New York now, finalizing the plans. We're to leave in a few weeks. I've known about this for weeks, but I've done nothing. I haven't found a doctor who could take over my practice. I haven't done a damn thing, and Dana comes home tomorrow."

"Because you don't want to go."

"Because I don't want to go," Jackie repeated. "And I should have told her before she left for New York. But an hour from now, I'll have changed my mind again and think I want to go. I keep squirming around like a trapped snake." Jackie stopped as she looked at Dana's picture. "Dana is kind and generous. Thoughtful and warm. Gentle but passionate about her work. When you see pictures she has taken of people — the peddler on the street or the vegetable stand woman — the vulnerability of their souls comes out in her pictures. And now she's making all these plans, and I don't want to be a part of them. I feel sad and angry." Frustrated, Jackie got up. "Would you like more coffee?" she said to break the tension.

"No thanks. I'm fine."

Jackie picked up her cup and went into the kitchen. "This is a real conundrum, and I only have myself to blame." She raised her voice so Joni could hear her from the kitchen.

"How's that?" Joni studied Dana's picture. She tried to sense the same feeling that Jackie had described of a kind and generous woman. But all she could see was a beautiful woman with ravishingly beautiful green eyes. Joni felt her brown eyes pale by comparison. This is ridiculous, Joni said to herself. I am reacting to a picture. A picture of a woman I've met only briefly. Joni tried to assess all the emotions that were dashing through her mind. She leaned forward so she could study the picture. What was she feeling? Not jealousy. That was too strong an emotion. Regret. For the first time since Alex had died, she had found a place that made her feel safe, and now the woman who was responsible for that safety was thinking of leaving. Stop it, she mentally berated herself.

"Because I should have told her immediately. But I've been afraid to." Jackie carried her steaming cup of coffee back into the living room and sat down. "I didn't want to hurt her feelings."

"But you've got to tell her."

"Yes, and tomorrow."

"Can I be the devil's advocate?"

"Have at it."

Joni paused, uncertain she wanted to articulate her thoughts. If her argument was convincing, Jackie might agree. Do the right thing, her brain kept telling her. "Why not go," she blurted out. "It sounds like a really exotic place. Would you be able to practice medicine there?"

"Absolutely. She has even arranged for me to work in a clinic. But that's not what I want. And it's taken me this long to figure it out. It's not just practicing medicine that's important to me. It's practicing here where I've been doing it for the past umpteen years. I came back here because I thought I could make a difference. And together Vera and I started with this tiny little office and it's grown into a clinic. A clinic where my patients trust that they will be seen by someone who really cares about them. I admit, the caseload has grown and, as I said, it's time to bring in another doctor, but I want a doctor who will augment and complement what we've built so far. I know we could get one of the rent-a-doc services to send in someone to cover the clinic for a few months until the Board of Directors could find a replacement for me, but I don't want to do that. I would feel as if I'd been . . ." Jackie reflected, "surgically excised from a place that I love." She paused. A blanket of guilt enveloped her. She felt dejected. She had finally put into words what had been suppressed by nights of fiery lovemaking with Dana. "It's funny. Yesterday my dearest friend Kristan and I talked about this same thing and I was resolved that I wasn't going to go and that Dana would understand. Today . . ." Jackie scratched the top of her head. "I feel guilty having to tell her. The mind does love to play around with us."

"Or we like to play around with our minds?"

"Maybe." Jackie grimaced.

"When are you going to tell her?"

"She gets home tomorrow. I want to delay it, but I can't."

"No, you can't because it's not fair to you or to her." Joni thought about what she was saying. She felt relief. She frowned. That's what she was feeling, relief. Relief that Jackie planned to stay. "But maybe she already knows."

"Why do you say that?"

"I don't know. I think that when two people are really close, we say more by what we don't say than by what we do." Joni frowned. "Did that come out right?"

"It made sense to me," Jackie smiled for the first time. "Possibly, I don't know. Before she left for New York, there was a tentativeness to her leaving. I think she wanted to ask. Oh god," Jackie groaned. "What a mess. I don't want to hurt her."

"If you go you'll hurt her."

"I don't think so. Really it's only for three years, and I could make it work; I'm sure I can." Even Jackie could hear how unconvincing she sounded. "I'm vacillating again," she groaned.

"You're a doctor, not an actress. Dana would sense your unhappiness and feel guilty. If she's the type of person you've described, she wouldn't be happy unless you were."

"No, she's too kind. I hope you can get to know her before she leaves. But time is so critical right now. She's supposed to be in Greece right around the first of July."

"A little more than a month. You're right. If you decide to stay here, time is going to be so compressed for you. Don't invite anyone else into your lives," Joni said reflectively. "Just grab hold of the time you have and jealously shelter it from everything else."

Jackie leaned both of her arms back over her head and stretched. The kinks she felt along her spine she knew were exacerbated by the tension she felt in her muscles. "Such wisdom. Thank you."

Joni traced the seam on her running pants. "You're welcome."

"And what about you? Why is Joni Coan living in Bailey's Cove?"

Joni looked over at the clock on Jackie's mantel. "It's ten o'clock?" There was surprise in her voice. "I've got to be going." She stood up. Joni's smile was impish. "I'd offer to hug you, but that's how this all started."

Jackie put her head back and laughed. "You're right." She stood up and held out her hand. "But I can say thank you." Joni put her hand in Jackie's, their touch warm. "This really helped. I hadn't planned to talk about my life problems. Really."

"I know. I'm just glad I was here to listen. Well," Joni said putting her hands inside her jacket pocket. She was surprised at how much she had wanted to touch Jackie. "I'll see you at the clinic tomorrow. Hope it goes well tomorrow night. I've found that the telling part is always the hardest."

"Yeah, especially when it involves your own life." They were standing at the door. "Thank you for listening."

"Thank you for telling me." Jackie was drawn to the sincerity in Joni's eyes.

"Somehow," Jackie said quietly. "I suspect a lot of people trust telling you things." She looked deep into Joni's eyes. "Thank you."

Chapter 10

Monday dragged. There were patients and rounds, but the day felt like a never-ending slow waltz. Joni had been quiet and attentive to detail. Carin seemed downright garrulous and overly friendly. Jackie thought about the day as she was driving home. It was funny, every time she had turned around, Carin was there absolutely effervescent about the dinner at her house. She'd overheard her telling Joni and Vera about their Sunday evening. The telling made it sound like more fun than what had actually happened. Jackie looked at her watch. She'd already picked up Bob, and there was enough time to feed her and shower before Dana got home. As she turned off the road, Jackie saw the rented car parked in her driveway and Dana watching from the door. She let Bob out of the backseat and watched as the dog ran over to her favorite spot and squatted. Dana walked out of the house and into Jackie's arms.

"I just got here. I've missed you," she whispered against Jackie's lips. Their tongues burned with passion.

"I've missed you," Jackie said between kisses. She rested her nose against Dana's neck and inhaled the spiciness of her perfume. How could she tell her she didn't want to move to Greece? Jackie closed her eyes and willed herself to feel happy about the future.

"Come on." Jackie felt Dana's breathlessness. "I've got something to give you." They held hands as they walked in the house.

"What?"

"This." Dana handed her the wrapped package.

"What is it?"

"You don't have to guess, just open it."

Jackie fumbled with the taped end and reached for a knife. She sliced through the tape and pulled the brown paper off. She stopped as she looked at the picture.

"It's a montage of pictures I've taken of us in the past three years. I had a friend of mine put it together in New York. He made one for you and one for me."

Jackie traced a finger around the outline of the faces. How many times had Dana set her camera on a rock to capture them on the beach. There was a picture of them on the skiing trip last year to Sugarloaf. She smiled. There was even a picture of her asleep in the hammock. "You know." It was a statement.

"I've known from the first night. Actually, I've known for a year now. Each time I've returned, it has been harder to reconnect. We consume each other for weeks, but we're never sated. I'm not referring to our nights. I mean our days. I thought three years in Greece would make a difference. Yet, I was angry at you because I knew you'd never leave and angry at me because I realized how much I really wanted that job.

I had to sign because I . . ." She touched the photographs, and Jackie sensed her hesitancy. "This is our history. That's why I had it made. We've had some perfect moments." Dana looked up at Jackie through tears.

"I'm so sorry." Jackie wiped the tears that were rolling down Dana's cheeks with her thumbs. "I'm so very sorry. I wish I could change who I am. I wish I could pretend to want this, but I can't. I've tried, but I can't."

"I know. I don't regret for a moment falling in love with you. And you know what's funny? I'm always going to be in love with you. It's just that we both love who we are in that world out there," Dana said gently. "And that's what we can't escape. And I'm sorry for crying. I kept telling myself I wouldn't all the way back on the plane."

"Don't be." Jackie folded Dana into her arms. "I love you and I'll always love you. God, we only have a few weeks left."

"No, we only have tonight. I changed my reservation. I can't prolong this. It's rational and logical, but painful. We need to start tomorrow now, but tonight I want to make love. I want to make love as if it is the first time and the last time."

Jackie kissed Dana. She licked the tears from Dana's eyes and tasted the saltiness of her sadness. "I don't want this to end like this, not with sadness."

"No, not with sadness." Dana reached up and pulled Jackie's mouth hard against her. "Only with passion," she said against her lips.

The next few weeks, Jackie thought of as her mechanical woman days. The Fourth of July had come and gone, and Jackie remembered little of it. Kristan and Jennifer were together again, but she sensed the distance between them. Kristan looked relieved, but Jennifer's face had stress lines that hadn't been there before.

Weekends were the most painful because she was alone.

She couldn't resist playing the music she and Dana had shared, Brian Adams, Celine Dion. Songs that talked about a constant love. After playing them, she was determined to dump the CDs in the trash and never listen to them again, but she couldn't bring herself to take them out of the stereo. Instead, she'd angrily snap off the stereo, put on her jacket, and take a long walk on the beach.

In the past a walk on the beach had been a mild sedative, calming her jangled nerves. But not this time. Even Bob offered little distraction. Instead of watching Bob, she'd reach into her pocket for the locket Dana had given her on their first Valentine's Day together. On one side was a picture of Dana, and on the other a picture of her. They were smiling across the tiny gold frames at each other.

Try as she would, she could not stop the tears. Stinging, hot, angry tears. Dana had called only once to say she had arrived safely in Greece. Several times Jackie had reached for the telephone to call her, but her arm felt like it had a drag anchor attached to it.

She knew that Dana had talked to Vera, because Vera had let it slip, but lately Vera had been silent. Funny, Jackie thought, since Dana had left, everyone and everything at the clinic seemed muted. Even Carin had retreated from her usual happy self.

Eventually, weekends gave way to Mondays, and she flooded herself with work. She spent more time at the hospital making rounds and longer hours at the clinic finishing her paperwork, routines that helped her get through the days but that in no way compensated for the loneliness of the nights.

"Can I come in?" Vera was subdued as she stepped into Jackie's office.

"Of course."

"We need to talk."

"There's nothing to talk about," Jackie snapped.

Vera stared at the diplomas behind Jackie's head. She ignored Jackie's mood. "I can't take away the pain. I'm not even going to pretend that I can." Vera looked intently at her. "But just remember, you two came to the same decision because it was the only one."

"In my sensible moments I realize that." She was less caustic. "But at night that decision seems pretty shaky. We spent months apart and we adjusted, but this is so permanent."

"Jackie, don't rethink it. Dana and you met, fell in love, but it wasn't a lifetime commitment. Look, I love my niece dearly and I think I know her better than anyone, including you. Don't" — Vera held up her hand to stop Jackie's objection — "Dana was never meant to be a lifelong commitment. She wasn't like Marianne. And that's what you wanted her to be. You and Marianne fell in love and you became the center of her life and she yours. That's how it's supposed to work. But Dana was different. She fell in love with you, but you were never the center of her life," Vera said kindly. "She loved who she was more. And if you had gone to Greece with her, you'd have spent weeks alone. She is traveling all over the country. Taking pictures here, there. What would you have done, sat and waited for her?"

"Yes. No. I don't know." Jackie felt the tears burning her eyes.

"Jackie, you're grieving for something you never had. You and Dana had . . ." Vera stopped. "You had a three-year date. That's what you're mourning."

"You can't possibly grasp what it is I'm feeling," Jackie snapped. She bit her bottom lip. "I'm sorry. This is a lousy way to channel my anger. Vera, I'm really sorry." Jackie looked at her longtime friend. "I'm sorry," she said humbly. "Someday I know I will be able to absorb what you're saying to me. But right now I miss her." Jackie wiped the tears off her cheeks. "I miss her."

"I know," Vera sighed. "Dana had a way of infiltrating everyone's heart. I'm not saying she didn't love you, that she doesn't still love you. It's just that it's like trying to cage a bird. She'd never have been happy living here, and you'd never been happy living there."

"I know, and those moments when I'm not angry at her or myself, I know what you're saying. But it doesn't make this time any easier. I've been a grizzly."

"Yes, you have." Vera smiled for the first time. "I'm glad you can say it. Everyone is holding her breath around you, even Carin. But that's another matter."

"What does that mean?" Jackie frowned at Vera, "Has Carin done something?" Jackie sat forward in her chair. "She's been very kind to me lately. Getting my coffee, offering to do things."

"That's what I'm worried about." Vera inhaled deeply. "I called Sondra."

Jackie looked at her office manager for the first time. "Why? I don't need a physical exam."

"I asked her if she could help us out for a few months."

"Why?" Jackie said with more intensity.

"We need some help around here. You've been adding more patients. This is not about Dana; this is about you. For some time now, I've been thinking about this, and I feel the time is right. She's due for a sabbatical from Harvard. She seemed excited about the prospect. She's worked here before, and the patients love her. She's a good doctor. It was ironic because I called her to ask her to recommend somebody, and she said she would love to do it. Said she and Jamie had been talking about where they wanted to go during her sabbatical. You know her specialty is rural medicine. They'd talked about Alaska, but Sondra actually got excited when I suggested she spend the year here."

"Don't you think you've taken on a little more responsibility than has been given you?" Jackie found that she lacked the energy to get angry at Vera.

"Absolutely." Jackie noted that her office manager was unrepentant. "But someone had to decide, and it wasn't going to be you. It's been a busy summer, and we haven't even started into the flu season. I don't want to see you add stress to everything else that is going on in your life."

Jackie leaned back in her chair and thought about her longtime friend. They had trained at Mass General together. She and Marianne and Sondra Ophelia Stern and her partner, Jamie Hennessy, had been inseparable friends. When Marianne died, Sondra had taken her sabbatical from Harvard University and spent a year at the clinic while Jackie pulled her life together. The last time they had talked, Sondra had mentioned that she was due for another year's sabbatical, but she and Jamie were going to spend it in Alaska. Jackie had teased her about having a *Northern Exposure* television experience, but she also knew her friend loved rural medicine, said it was the only place where a doctor really is challenged.

"And, I've decided to make Joni senior nurse."

Jackie blinked. "What prompted that?"

"She's good and, frankly, I think we need to have a head nurse right now. Carin has taken advantage of the fact that you're upset and is bossing Joni around. Some lines need to be drawn. I think she'll listen to Joni, or I hope she will. Also, she won't listen to me."

"What do you mean Carin's bossing Joni and won't listen to you?" Jackie felt as though her mind had been in a fog.

Vera held up her hands. "Nothing serious. Just on occasion I've heard her telling Joni to do things. And as far as I'm concerned, I've asked her to work over and she won't. She's seemed disturbed lately. And . . ." Vera hesitated. "I don't like the way she's been making excuses to hang around you. Getting you coffee and fabricating reasons to be in the office. I don't know. I just think we need to put Joni in charge. May I ask what does she talk about?"

Jackie rubbed her eyes with the palms of her hands. "Frankly, I haven't paid that much attention. She seems to talk a lot about herself." She leaned back in her chair and chuckled. "You've been busy. Actually," she said more seriously as she thought about Sondra, "I don't have the energy to argue with you. Do what you want."

Vera stood up. "Good."

"Good. Now that you've organized my professional life, any suggestions about my personal life?"

"Why don't you ask Joni to dinner tonight? Tell her you've decided to make her senior nurse. Tell her about Sondra. I think that would be a good idea and good for you."

"What's up that puffy black sleeve of yours?" Jackie asked suspiciously.

Vera smoothed the sleeve down on her jacket. "Nothing, just that you need to get out and that this would be the right time to tell her about the changes. Enlist her support. She's a good nurse, Jackie, and I suspect she would be a very good friend."

"Okay, okay," Jackie held up her hands. "Stop the kibitzing. I'll ask her if she'd like to have dinner and tell her about your plans, not my plans."

"Whatever." Vera had her hand on the doorknob. "I just want you to go out and do something besides sit at home and feel sorry for yourself. By the way, you have five minutes, and then you need to be at the hospital to make rounds." Vera stepped out the door before Jackie had a chance to respond.

Jackie shook her head. Vera was impishly incorrigible, but Jackie knew that the woman had a great capacity to love and that Vera was being a friend more than an office manager. She slipped on her white lab coat and looked in the mirror. She was startled at the face that looked back. The face looked tired.

Jackie discovered that she was looking forward to dinner. Vera had made all the arrangements, including reservations for seven o'clock. Jackie smiled to herself. For the first time in years, it felt good to have someone else take charge of her life. Vera was just what the doctor had ordered. She was just reaching for her jacket when she heard a knock on her door. She wondered if Joni had changed her mind about dinner.

"Come in?"

"Hi." Carin closed the door behind her and stood just inside. "Can I talk with you?"

"Of course." Jackie motioned to a chair.

"I'd rather stand if it's okay."

"Is something wrong?" Jackie noticed the red eyes.

"Oh . . . I . . ." Carin's chin began to quiver. Jackie wasn't sure how it had happened, but Carin was one moment standing at the door and the next leaning against her, crying on her shoulder.

"What's wrong?" Jackie put her hands on the woman's shoulders and eased her into a chair. She handed her some Kleenex.

"Just that Darrel and I had a fight, and I don't think Vera likes me." The words rushed out between sobs.

"What makes you think Vera doesn't like you?"

"Just that she seems to always be talking privately with Joni, and when I try to talk with her she acts like she doesn't have time. I've tried to be so nice to her," she said between sniffles. "I've even invited her to have dinner with Darrel and me."

"Well," Jackie said. "Vera certainly has never even hinted that she disliked you. She's been extra busy lately. I couldn't run this office without her. But she's really a very nice person." Jackie hesitated. She was uncertain how deeply she wanted to delve into the woman's personal problems, nor did she feel she had the energy to deal with one more issue, but the words were out of Carin's mouth before she could even ask.

"I just wanted to be friends with her, what with Darrel and me fighting all the time. He's just being a man." Her voice took on an assertive tone. "I told him there was nothing to be jealous of, but he just keeps going on and on. Last night, I told him to shut up and leave me alone. He stormed out. That's never happened before."

"I don't understand. What's he jealous of?"

"You?"

"Me?" Jackie felt her stomach tighten.

"Well, yes." Carin dabbed at her eyes with the Kleenex and blew her nose. "Excuse me," she said. She balled up the Kleenex and moved it from hand to hand. "He said I'm always talking about you. Said I never seem to have time for him. I told him he was just being silly. Said you and I were just friends and that friends like to talk."

Jackie picked up her wastebasket and held it out so Carin could drop the Kleenex inside.

"Thank you."

"Carin." Jackie cleared her throat. "You and I . . . have a working relationship. You're a good nurse, and I value your work here in the office, but really . . . Would you like me to speak with Darrel?" she asked tentatively.

"Holy cow, no. He'd go ballistic. Please don't do that, Jackie . . . I mean, Doctor. I can handle it." Carin stood up and backed toward the door. "Really, I can handle Darrel. He's just out of sorts. Been working a lot lately. Really," she said again.

"I just want to help smooth things over for you. It seems the two of you have a very nice marriage."

"Really, uh, I think it's fine. I'm sorry I got so upset." Carin opened the door and closed it quickly behind her.

Jackie sat staring at the closed door. Vera was right — she'd been in too much of a brain drain lately. She picked up her medical bag. She had been a doctor for more than twenty-five years and yet was still surprised to learn that people can't be placed in a box and categorized.

It constantly amazed her the level of value people attached to relationships. There were people in Bailey's Cove who referred to her as their friend, yet she'd never once been to their home. It was clear Carin was looking for a friend; maybe Joni could help. But it was not her job to pick or even to suggest to Joni whom she should befriend. Funny, she thought as she got into her car, Joni was someone she was looking forward to getting to know as a friend, and somehow she got the feeling that Joni attached the same values to their relationship as she did.

Chapter 11

Joni thought again about her conversation with Vera as she prepared for dinner with Jackie. They had talked about her promotion, but Joni had said she wanted to think about it. She was excited that a new doctor was joining the staff, even if for only a year.

But she knew that it would be her job to deal with Carin, and she wasn't certain she wanted that responsibility. She studied her face in the mirror. Sturdy. That was how people described her. Her mother had called her *salt of the earth*. One time she looked that phrase up in her thesaurus and discovered terms like *stout fellow, brick, rough diamond, ugly duckling,* and *white man*. She chuckled to herself. Somehow that put everything into perspective, especially the white man part.

As she slipped on her black skirt and smoothed it down over her hips, she thought about Jackie. She empathized with the pain the doctor was going through. Even though she suspected that the decision to remain behind had been mutual, Joni knew there was no antidote for the withdrawal pains Jackie was feeling. She wondered if Jackie was rethinking her decision. Joni hoped not; she really enjoyed working with her. The past few weeks had been more difficult, because Jackie had been downright stoic and at times maniacal when it came to work. She buttoned her red silk blouse. Pain does pass; it's just the remembrance of pain that lingers, she thought. She looked at herself in her full-length mirror and realized she was dressed up. "Fool, woman," she said out loud to the image. "This is not a dinner date. This is a business meeting."

She went back in the bathroom and reached for her lipstick. She leaned closer to the mirror and traced the lipstick across her full lips. She tore off a piece of toilet paper, blotted her lips, and tossed the paper into the toilet. Water absorbed the pink lips, and the tissue floated to the bottom. She pulled on a matching black jacket and brushed hair from the collar. She walked into the bedroom and looked at herself again in the full-length mirror. She loved to wear skirts and dresses, but Alex used to tease her about how un-lesbian it was. She wasn't crazy about what floated back at her. She turned left, then right. It looked like she had added a few pounds around her hips.

She'd never hated her full-figure look because Alex said that was what she had fallen in love with, but lately she seemed to be surrounded by women who offered smooth lines and curvaceous hips. Alex had made her feel beautiful.

Joni sat down on the bed, her thoughts ponderously heavy. They'd been together ten years, but the last two had been tenuous after Alex's heart attack. A viral infection had changed their lives. Although Joni had worried and fretted, Alex battled hard against the restricted activity, the diet, and the endless trips to specialists. Joni closed her eyes. What's the point, Alex would say, if we can't have fun. Joni put her head in her hands as she remembered the horror of the last week, the second heart attack and the seemingly endless tubes and monitors. There had been a minute of hope when they thought they had a replacement heart, but in the end Alex didn't match.

Afterward, she sat in her kitchen, clutching the socks Alex had worn at the hospital. She thought she'd never stop crying. Two months later, she quit the hospital. Too many memories. Each time she saw a family waiting anxiously for information about a family member, she found she couldn't tell them without crying.

Joni stood up and dabbed perfume behind her ears and on her wrists. Once again, she thought, she was playing solitaire with her memories, and she felt the loneliness. It had been a long time since the blackness had been this invasive. That's the last time she was going to think about her hips she thought as she smoothed her hair. After Alex's death, she never knew which thought or word would release the demons from their dungeon. Leaving Boston had been a temporary move, but Joni had been relieved when Vera hired her.

She thought about Jackie again. How odd that she and Jackie both had lost someone that had been the very center of their being. From what she had gleaned from some of the things Vera had told her, Jackie was absolutely devastated after Marianne's death. Vera had mentioned her one day when they were alone and was talking about the early days when Jackie had started the clinic. It was then that Joni realized that Marianne had been a nurse and had been at Jackie's side when she opened the clinic. Then Marianne had found a lump in her breast. Vera related the trips to Bangor and the months of agony Marianne had suffered through. Then the chemotherapy and radiation treatments. After that Jackie was alone.

It was during those alone years that Dana had entered her life. Joni had noted how taciturn Vera became when she talked about her niece. Joni frowned. As much as she tried to picture Jackie and Dana together, the snapshot just didn't want to coalesce. Dana seemed so unright for Jackie. "Stop that," she scolded. "Next thing you know," she groused at herself, "you'll want to pick out the doctor's partners."

She looked at the clock. Seven. She was late. She quickly buttoned her jacket, grabbed her keys and purse, and hurried to her car. Even though she tried to put a brake on her musing, she thought about Jackie again as she drove toward the restaurant. In the past few days, she realized that Jackie reminded her of Alex. Alex's love had been steadfast, and Joni sensed that same profundity in Jackie. She had observed Jackie's eyes those times Dana had been in the office, and Joni had been surprised at the depth of her reaction to what she'd seen. She'd felt irritated by Dana. At first the emotion had bothered her deeply, until she'd been able to fix the limits of it in her mind. It wasn't that she was in love with Jackie. She was certain that that wasn't possible. How could she love Jackie when she was still so in love with Alex? But, she thought, there was no question she had an affection for the woman. Jackie had Alex's same gentle manner and titanic capacity to show love. She realized she was rankled because Dana had had it all and had tossed it all away like attic junk. What a fool Dana had been, Joni thought. What a damn fool.

Jackie's car was in the parking lot, and Joni hurried into the restaurant. Jackie was talking with the owner. Joni inhaled deeply and felt tiny beads of perspiration under her lip. She wiped them away with her finger.

"Hi," Joni said. "I hope I haven't kept you waiting."

"Not at all." Jackie smiled. "Jim and I were just talking about golf."

"You play golf?"

"Show me a doctor that doesn't," Jackie laughed. "Come on. Jim says we can have the same table we had last time. You look very nice."

"Thank you." Joni felt slightly disconcerted by the compliment. She hesitated to return one, even though she liked Jackie's blue slacks and light blue blouse. She was carrying her jacket over her shoulder. She's your boss, remember, Joni said to herself.

"Vera suggested that we have dinner," Jackie said after they were seated. "And I've learned never to argue with Vera. Anyway" — she folded her hands together and looked directly at Joni — "I'm glad you could join me."

"Thank you."

Betty walked up to the table carrying a bottle of Beringer's White Zinfandel. "Good evening, Jackie, Joni, I'm so glad you could join us." Betty put two glasses on the table and poured.

Jackie looked questioningly from the wine bottle to Betty.

"Compliments of Vera," the waitress said as she set the bottle on the table.

Jackie and Joni laughed. "It doesn't look as though I'm going to escape her," Jackie said.

"No, it doesn't. She's really a magnificent woman. She's everyone's aunt, mother, and grandmother rolled into one," Joni added. "What I find most intriguing is how people relate to her. You're often in the examining room when patients come in, but I hear them talking to her. She's so willing to listen to their problems, whether they are medical or personal. I've heard people telling her the most intimate details of their lives, and they do it within those few moments while they are waiting to see you."

"I know," Jackie replied as she thought about her friend. "She always provides some level of stability to your life whether she solves your problem or not. But do you know what is most interesting?"

"What's that?"

"When we spend time together, we talk about me or other people, but never about you. Tell me about Nurse Joni."

"There's really not much to tell. I think we've covered most of the basics. Growing up here, nursing school, life after nursing school," she said wistfully.

"What about life after nursing school?"

After a vivid white instant of a smile, Joni said, "Not much to tell."

"Ah," Jackie sipped her wine. "It seems to me that now that I'm going to promote you to senior nurse, I need to know a little more about you." Jackie watched for any kind of reaction. "Vera told you."

"Yes." Joni laughed, diffusing some of her embarrassment. "I was supposed to act surprised when you told me, but I'm afraid I'm not very good at that. She asked me today if you were to offer me the job would I take it."

"And what did you say?"

"At first I said no."

"And now?"

"I say maybe," Joni's eyes were luminous.

"What changed your mind?"

"I've had an opportunity to think about it, and —"

"Well, I thought that was your car in the parking lot," Carin said to Jackie. "Mind if I join you? Darrel's having dinner with the boys, and I just hate eating alone."

Jackie looked at Joni and noticed a slight shrug. "Please join us," she said to Carin.

"Why, isn't this just wonderful." Carin sat next to Jackie at the table. "We should do this more often, just the three of us. We have so much in common. I'll just have a teensy bit of wine, 'cause I'm driving," she said to Betty, who set another wineglass on the table. "I haven't had a chance to even look at the menu. Have you two ordered?"

"No. Why don't you give us just a few more minutes, Betty, and we'll be ready," Jackie said.

"Why, this is such a coincidence," Carin said again. "So what were you two talking about?"

"I don't remember." Jackie said. "Do you?"

"No," Joni said. "I guess it wasn't all that important."

The rest of the evening was awash in stories about Darrel and growing up in Atlanta. Joni noticed that even though Carin said she only wanted a "teensy" bit of wine, she finished off the first bottle and ordered a second. Each story Carin told added to the colossal headache Joni had, and each word felt like an ice pick slamming against the side of her head.

"You know," Carin slurred to Jackie. "Joni and I have gotten to be just such good friends." She laid her hand on Jackie's arm and left it there. Joni watched as Jackie pulled her arm away. "Why at the clinic, we just laugh and giggle about everything."

"That's great." Jackie motioned for Betty. "Check, please."

"I have it ready." Betty looked down at Carin, who was drinking more wine as she handed the check to Jackie. "I can take that for you." Betty waited as Jackie reached for her credit card. "Would you like to sign this at the bar?"

Jackie looked at the waitress for the first time. "If you'd like. Excuse me," she said to Joni.

"Sure, sure, Jackie, take your time. Joni and I'll just talk about women things."

Joni watched as Jackie accompanied Betty to the bar and signed the credit slip. She wasn't paying any attention to Carin until she heard her say, "Yes, I think Jackie likes me a lot."

"What makes you say that?"

Carin leaned across the table. "Today, I was in her office and she —"

"Ready ladies?"

"Absolutely," Carin said. "Jackie, why don't you stop at my house for a nightcap?" She pursed her lips. "I expect Joni's going to want to get home."

"Actually, I think we've all had enough nightcaps. In fact, what I was going to suggest is," Jackie looked helplessly at Joni, "would you drive Carin's car? I'll follow you and bring you back."

"Oh, you don't need to do that. Why you could just drop me off, Jackie. That way Joni won't have to stay up any later."

"Come on, Carin. One thing I've learned over the years, never argue with the boss." Joni impatiently grabbed the woman by the arm and walked her through the restaurant.

Joni watched Jackie in her rearview mirror as she followed Carin's car. She ignored Carin's chatter. It was so easy to tune this woman out, especially after she had been drinking. When they had walked out to the parking lot, Carin had refused to give her her car keys, but when Jackie held out her hand, Carin giggled and slid them in her hand. When Joni pulled into Carin's driveway, she noticed Darrel's truck. Carin bumped against the car as she got out.

"I just want to say," she said to Jackie, "I had a wonderful time. And we must do this again." Carin reached for Jackie's hand.

"I'll walk her to the door." Joni firmly grabbed ahold of Carin's arm. She noted the look of relief on Jackie's face.

The porch light went on just as they reached the step. "Hi, honey. Glad you're home. This here's my friend Joni."

Darrel opened the screen door at the same time he reached out an arm to steady his wife. He looked over at Jackie. "Bye, darlings," Carin yelled. "I just love my boss . . ." Joni heard Carin say as the screen door closed behind her.

"It's been quite a night," Joni said as Jackie drove them back toward the restaurant.

"I'll say. Look, I'm sorry. This is not what was supposed to happen."

"I know."

"Would you like a cup of coffee or something?"

"Ordinarily, I'd say yes, but I have this mammoth headache, and I'm afraid I wouldn't be very good company."

"Look, I'm truly sorry."

"This wasn't your fault," Joni said quietly. "But the one who is going to be most disappointed is Vera." Joni watched as the telephone poles whipped past her. They reminded her of a sinuous rhythm, and she found it comforting and downright hypnotic.

"You're right! I was supposed to talk to you about the job offer."

"Look," Joni held up her hand. "Vera talked with me earlier. I told her I'd think about it. This incident with Carin has changed my mind; I'll accept."

"Carin could be a continuing problem. There's something going on there I don't understand."

"Well, I think I do. There are people who need to be central to all the attention, and I think she's one of them. I don't mean that unkindly. I just think it's true."

"Interesting that she should happen to turn up at a restaurant where we were going to have dinner. That's twice now."

"I wonder how happenstance it was."

"I don't understand." Jackie turned into the parking lot and parked near Joni's car.

"I suspect she might have overheard Vera talking to me." Joni shrugged. Her head was pounding. "Or maybe I'm just being paranoid. Anyway, don't ask me why, but I'll take the job."

Jackie smiled. "Good."

"Of course, Carin won't like it, especially since I didn't come to work until after her, but she'll get over it. By the way, were you and the waitress talking about her?"

"Yes. Jim was concerned about her driving home. Said if I wanted he would take the keys from her and see that she got home. I told Betty she was my responsibility. What with all the liability that places like that have, I can understand his concern."

"I can too," Joni said as she opened the door of the car. "I'm really looking forward to the new doctor joining us. Vera said she's a friend of yours."

"Yes, Sondra and I were at Mass General together. We've been friends a long time."

"As I said, I accept the job and can assure you that although the idea seemed pretty incongruous at first, after tonight I wouldn't think of turning you down."

"I'm not sure I understand." Jackie frowned.

"Someday I'll explain it to you, but not tonight. My head is throbbing, and all I want to do is go home and go to bed."

"I'd like to tell you that it was a pleasant evening, but I don't think you'd believe it."

"It was for a while." Joni smiled. "Good night, Jackie."

Jackie waited until she got out of the car. "Would you like to have dinner this weekend?"

"Yes, I would. But with one proviso."

"What's that."

"We have it at my house." She smiled back at Jackie. "And the only other female I want you to bring is Bob. I suspect Carin's going to have a hard time running into us there."

Jackie grinned. "You're on."

Chapter 12

Jackie set her medical journal aside and watched Bob, who was hard at work chewing on her latest toy. She reminded Jackie of a beaver as she gnawed her way around the toy. All around her were other half-chewed toys that she'd discarded.

It had been an interesting few weeks, she thought. Carin had seemed at first surprised and then acceptant of Joni's new status. Sondra had called, and she and Jamie would be in Bailey's Cove in about three weeks. She and Kristan had been on the telephone a lot. Although Jennifer was back, things were still tenuous between them. Today Kristan had asked her to speak with Jennifer, and Jackie had called Jennifer's office. Jennifer said she would stop at Jackie's house on the way home. When Jackie warned her that she didn't get home until late because of hospital rounds, Jennifer said she worked late into the evening, so she'd stop by after work. Jackie knew that Jennifer didn't stay late at the office unless she had a big trial. So Jackie knew that was a new pucker in Kristan and Jennifer's relationship. In the past, Kristan and Jennifer couldn't wait to get home. Jackie looked at the time; Jennifer would be there any minute. Time to turn on the coffeepot, she thought. She stood up and continued to watch Bob's antics. She started to reach for one of the toys to toss it when the telephone rang. "Hello."

"Hi."

Jackie sucked in her breath. "How are you?" She could feel her heart racing.

"Fine. You?"

"Fine. I'm sorry I haven't called. I've been in a remote section of the country on a shoot."

"That's okay."

"Jackie. I called to —"

"I know." Jackie pushed her free hand through her hair. "I expected you'd be busy over there. Especially at first."

"Well, you were right. I haven't had a free moment." Dana paused. "I miss you."

Jackie closed her eyes. She didn't want the conversation to go in this direction. It had been a difficult few weeks and she just now felt that she had command of her emotions. "Any new projects?"

"You don't want to talk about it, do you?"

"Not particularly."

"Have you missed me at all?"

Jackie paused. "Dana, it's been a rotten few weeks. I'm sure it's been lousy for you, too. But I really don't want to talk about it. I really don't."

"Can you so compartmentalize your life that you don't want to at least talk through some of the emotions we are feeling?" Jackie heard the petulance in Dana's voice for the first time.

She could feel her temperature climbing. "Talk through the emotions? Dana, I've been submerged in tears. Is that what you wanted to hear? Because it's not what I want to talk about."

"I just thought we'd be able to —"

Bob heard the car before she did and growled. "Easy watchdog."

"Is someone there?"

"Jennifer is stopping by."

"How are they?"

"Fine. Hang on." Funny, she thought as she set the telephone down, Jennifer usually did not knock. Jackie frowned when she saw Carin on the porch.

"Hi, Jackie. I was just in the neighborhood and thought I'd stop by."

Jackie stepped aside. She could smell the alcohol as Carin walked past her.

"Why, isn't this just lovely," Carin said as she walked around the kitchen. "Oh dear, you're on the telephone." She leaned against the kitchen cabinet. "Please finish."

Jackie looked from her to the telephone. "Hi," she picked up the receiver. "My nurse dropped by unexpectedly. I have to go."

"Convenient," Jackie could hear the doubt in Dana's voice. "Will you call me?"

"I don't know." Jackie watched Carin. She did not even pretend to not listen.

"Call me, please. And soon." Jackie heard the click even before she could answer.

"I didn't mean to interrupt." Carin smiled at her. "I just love country kitchens. And that view. I just bet that's beautiful during the day. When Darrel and I moved here, I just fell in love with a place in Bayport. Had an ocean view as pretty as yours. But we couldn't afford it. He said someday. I bet he will, his business keeps growing like it is. We might even live right here on the ocean in Bailey's Cove. Got anything to drink?" Carin sat down on a kitchen chair.

"Carin, I don't wish to seem rude, but a friend of mine will be here any minute. And we need to talk about some personal things, so I really —"

"Now, Jackie." Carin's voice sounded purposeful to Jackie. "I think you're just trying to get rid of me. Why, what a cute puppy. What's its name?"

"Bob. Look, Carin, a friend really is stopping by, and I need the time to speak with her privately."

"Well, I expect you might want to speak with me, too, Doctor," Jackie could hear the haughtiness in her voice. "I think you need to intervene with something at work, or it could turn a very bad situation into a tragedy." She looked around the kitchen. "How about a cup of coffee?"

Jackie sat down in the kitchen chair opposite Carin. "I don't have any made. What do you mean?"

"It's Vera, I think you have to reprimand her."

"Vera?"

"Yes, Vera. I told you before she doesn't like me, and she's gone ahead and promoted Joni over me. I'm really disappointed. Now she tells me another doctor is starting at the clinic."

"That's true. She'll be here in a few weeks."

"Well, don't you think someone should have told me?"

"Why?"

"Because I have a right to know what goes on where I work. I'll tell you, I think Vera and Joni are conspiring to get rid of me. They're always meeting and talking. Joni won't even have lunch with me anymore. Announced we were going to have staggered lunch hours. Why there's no one in the clinic during those hours."

"There will be. The other doctor and I plan to stagger our lunch hours so the office is always covered."

"That's what I mean. No one tells me anything," Carin complained. "They just announce something is going to happen. I don't like it."

"I'm sorry that decisions have been made and that you weren't in the loop. I'll speak with Vera about that."

"Well, that's better. But I want Joni fired. She's made my life hell for the past few weeks. Ordering me to do this or that."

"I haven't heard her order you to do anything."

"Well, you're not around when she does it," Carin whined. "She's tricky. She really is. Besides, after your friend left" — Carin leaned across the table and touched Jackie's hand — "I thought we'd get to be close friends."

Jackie pulled her hand away. "Carin, you work in my office. There's nothing else going on."

Carin rubbed her hand across her chest and down her arm. "I've never been with a woman before. It might be kind of fun. 'Course, I'd never tell Darrel. And it'd be fun for you, Jackie." Carin leaned across the table, her eyes drawing Jackie's to her. "Think of the fun of peeling away —"

Jackie and Carin heard the car at the same moment. Carin turned her head toward the door. "Is this one of your friends like Dana?" Carin chirped.

"Look, I'm going to overlook that remark because I know you've been drinking. I think you need to leave." Jackie kept her voice level.

Carin didn't move. "Well, I think, Doctor, that you've got a major decision to make. I want Vera reprimanded and Joni fired. I think I deserve that job and I want it." Jackie could see Carin trembling from anger. She was amazed at the range of emotions, from vamp to viper, the woman mastered in just seconds.

"Vera promoted Joni with my approval, so no one is going

to be reprimanded or fired, and I think you need to go home and sober up." Jackie heard the soft rap on her door and felt relieved to see Jennifer standing there. "Hi, come in," she told Jennifer.

Jennifer looked past Jackie. "Am I interrupting something?"

"No, my nurse was just leaving."

Carin patted her hair as she stood up. "I'm Carin Chase. Pleased to meet you," she said to Jennifer. "Maybe we should hug. Isn't that what girls do nowadays?"

Jennifer shook her hand but said nothing. She looked from Carin to Jackie.

"We'll talk about this tomorrow." Carin eyes narrowed as she looked at Jackie. "And I expect a resolution to this teensy-weensy problem. Nice meeting you," she said to Jennifer as she walked out.

"Wow. What was that all about?" Jennifer asked.

"I don't know." Jackie then related what had happened just minutes before Jennifer arrived. "Anyway, once she goes home and thinks about what she did, I expect she'll be sorry in the morning when she sobers up."

"I don't know. This may be just a lawyer talking, but I suggest you be careful, my friend. That's one angry lady. And I don't like the way she's coming on to you. Some women need validation at all levels. Is Joni gay?"

"I don't know. I get the feeling that she is, but we've never really talked about it. We've had dinner a few times. In fact, I spent a very pleasant evening with her last weekend, but we've just never talked about it. Funny, she rarely talks about herself."

"What do you talk about?"

"The office, things we've read, places we've been, those kinds of things. She has mostly listened to me lately talk about Dana. Funny, she tuned in very quickly that there was a problem. Which leads me to believe she may be gay or a truly nonhomophobic straight woman."

"I was really sorry to hear about Dana and you. There's no resolution?"

"No. In fact she was on the telephone when Carin arrived. Strange. She says she loves Greece and her new job. And you know" — Jackie set two cups on the table and reached for the coffeepot — "I'm happy for her. Sad for me, but happy for her." Jackie rubbed her temple. "But that's not what I wanted to talk with you about."

"I think I'd rather listen to your problems." Jennifer accepted the cup of coffee and sipped it. "At least you found some sort of resolution. What about another woman in your life?"

"Never. After Marianne and Dana, I don't think there's anyone who could fill my life. Marianne was my lover, soul mate, and friend. Dana was, well, Dana was just about the most exciting woman I've ever been with. Come on, let's sit in the living room. Is there no resolution for you and Kristan?" she said to change the subject.

"I don't know."

"What happened?"

"Didn't Kristan tell you?"

"Yes, but I'd like to hear how you saw that night." Jackie listened quietly as Jennifer related the night of the lobster dinner and her disappointment when she told Kristan about her meeting with Jackie and her desire to have a child. She talked about how hard it has been for her to think beyond the disappointment.

"Anyway, we're trying to work through it, but I don't know if I can. Isn't that strange." Jennifer rubbed her eyes.

Jackie noticed for the first time how much weight Jennifer had lost and how tired she looked.

"What about seeing a counselor?"

"Kristan suggested it, but I don't want to do that."

"Why not?"

"I don't think this can be fixed."

"Wait a minute. You're an intelligent and educated

woman. You know that unless you try, it certainly can't be fixed."

"Jackie, I described my reaction that night as disappointment, but it's bigger than that. I was mortified by what happened. I thought I was living with someone I understood completely. But I was wrong."

"But she wants to fix it."

"How do I trust the reason she wants to fix it? Does she want a child because she fears she will lose me or because she really wants one? I can't find any security in anything she tells me because I don't understand her motivation anymore."

"Can one mistake unravel everything?" Jackie scratched the back of her head.

"Yes, when it's of this magnitude." Jennifer set her glass on the table. "It's more than just her reaction. Kristan and I had a symbiotic relationship that's hard to attach words to. It's as though we could read each other's mind. She knew what I was thinking and I always knew what she was thinking, or at least I thought I did. But when it came to one of the most important things in the world for us to connect on, she was going in a different direction. And that's why we're where we are now. This isn't about disappointment; this is about peeling away levels of life with someone you thought you knew and finding that the excavation leads to a different path. That's what this is about. I haven't felt the same about her since, and I've tried, Jackie, I've really tried. The problem is me, not her."

"So what's the solution?"

"I don't know. She has suggested counseling, talking with you. She has suggested a vacation, a lot of things."

"And?"

"I find I have neither the inclination or the energy to do anything."

"So you just go on living together, existing?"

"I know one thing." Jennifer stared at Jackie. "My biological clock is ticking, and I want a child. I can't describe how important that is to me. I just don't know if I will want to do it with Kristan." Jennifer's voice broke.

Jackie held out her arms. "Come here," she said gently.

Jennifer leaned her head against Jackie's shoulder and sobbed. "I'm sorry," she hiccuped, "I thought I'd gotten past this part."

"It takes a long time to get past the tears." Jackie stroked Jennifer's hair. "Do you love Kristan?"

"Yes, but not like before. I'm" — Jennifer sat up and wiped her eyes on the back of her shirtsleeve — "I'm really really angry with her."

"But that's what you have to get past, Jennifer. Don't you understand that? Your distrust of Kristan may just be anger. You need to move beyond that. Otherwise you're going to end up building this huge emotional waste dump filled with anger in your brain, and there will be no way for you and Kristan to get past it." Jackie thought about how she wanted to say the words. "You know, after you and Kristan got together, I envied you." She held up her hand to stop Jennifer's objection. "In a way, a mild jealousy, I guess.

"Dana and I never shared that closeness, and I don't think we would have even if she hadn't been a thousand miles away most of the time. But Marianne and I had it. I think it's something that comes along once in a lifetime. When Marianne died, that part of my life died with her. Strange how death short-circuits so many things in our lives, but I count myself as one of the lucky. I know you find it hard to believe, but there are people who fall in love and live with someone for years, but they never find a soul mate. Marianne and I were soul mates, and you and Kristan are soul mates. But you guys have a choice, and you've got to make that choice, Jennifer. Otherwise . . . otherwise it'll never be the same. You may never again find what you had with Kristan."

"That's just what I'm afraid of." Jennifer sobbed. "That even after counseling we may never go back to what we had."

"But unless you try —"

"Jackie, I want a child. I do know that."

"Then have a child. But also try to put your relationship back together. I know a wonderful counselor who would talk with both of you."

Jennifer hesitated.

"Are you afraid of the future, or are you afraid of the counselor?"

"Both. I've never had much use for going to talk with a counselor. I don't know," Jennifer pushed the hair off her forehead and held her hands against her cheeks. "Why do you always feel feverish after crying?"

"Your blood pressure goes up and the blood rushes to your cheeks, but I don't think you're interested in a clinical definition."

"Have you and Kristan talked about this?"

"Yes, mostly on the telephone. Once face to face while you were in Portland."

"Would you be violating a confidence if you told me what she wants?"

"No, I don't think so. She wants you. Loves you desperately, can't and won't think of living without you."

"And the baby."

"She wants one desperately with you."

"Because she's afraid of losing me or because she truly wants one?"

Jackie sighed deeply. "I don't know. I really don't know, and I don't think Kristan knows. That's why I think a counselor would be good. She might help."

"Well, if she can't then nobody can, because we can't go on like this. I would rather —" Jennifer stopped. "Well, I would rather not say what I would rather —"

"I think I know."

Jennifer looked at the clock. "Yikes, it's ten o'clock. I've got to get going. I've loads of office work to finish."

Jackie frowned as she looked at the clock. "Can I ask one final question?"

"Shoot."

"Are you working late nights because you're preparing for a big case or because you're avoiding going home?"

Jennifer stared down at her feet. "It's avoidance."

"That won't fix it."

"I know, but I've found it much easier than trying to talk with Kristan. It's cowardly, but it seemed right."

"Go home, Jennifer, and go to a counselor. Here." She handed Jennifer a business card.

"You come prepared."

"Only when it comes to friends."

Jennifer hugged Jackie. "You're very special, my friend. I count you as a win in my life."

"I'm pretty lucky too. I count both you and Kristan as my closest friends. I would hate to see anything happen to you two."

"But if Kristan and I were to separate?"

"You'd still be my friend, you can count on that."

"Thanks, Jackie." Jennifer held the card up. "I'll call her tomorrow and make an appointment."

Jackie watched as Jennifer got into her car. How complicated life had become lately, she thought.

Chapter 13

An emergency at the hospital made Jackie late getting to the office, but when she arrived, she saw patients waiting in the lobby and her front office vacant of staff. She heard voices coming from her office, and when she looked in she found Vera and Joni.

"What's going on?" Jackie asked.

"It's a mess, Jackie, a Queen of England royal mess." Jackie could hear the frustration in Vera's voice.

Jackie put her black bag on a chair and sat down next to Vera. She looked questioningly at Joni.

"Carin's been in a rage all morning, and when Vera told her to go home," Joni said, "she yelled at her. Told her that you were going to reprimand her and fire me. I tried to calm her down, but she stormed out a few minutes ago, said she was going for coffee and she'd be back when you got here."

"She's demented, Jackie," Vera said matter-of-factly. "I've never been around anyone like her before."

"I can't figure it out. She came to my house last night a little blitzed and made demands, said she wanted you reprimanded and Joni fired. I told her to sleep it off. But I've been thinking about it since last night. I don't think she was drunk; I think she wanted me to think she was."

"What's going on?" Vera asked.

"I honestly don't know." She looked over at Joni. "Any ideas?"

"I think right now we need to get the office operating smoothly," Joni said quietly. "Vera, you pull the files and we'll get everyone set up in the examining rooms. When Carin comes in —"

"When Carin comes in, I'll deal with her." Jackie felt her impatience growing. She shook her head. Lately the quiet she had enjoyed in her personal and professional life had vanished. She wondered if her life would ever return to normal.

"May I make a suggestion?" Joni said tentatively.

"Of course."

"I don't think you should see her without either me or Vera there as a witness."

"I don't think she'd try to hurt me."

"Not physically, no. But given her mental state, I'm not sure what she'll do."

Jackie inhaled deeply and held her breath. She could feel the muscles tighten in her stomach. "Vera, go back to your desk and when she comes in, give me a heads up. I'll tell her I want to speak with her and, as her immediate supervisor," she said to Joni, "I want you to join us."

Vera patted Jackie's hand. "It'll be okay. Really."

"I can't see how it could get much worse than this. How'd we get to this? We used to have the most boring lives on the planet," the humor Jackie was reaching for fell flat.

"We will again," Vera said as she opened the door for Joni. Vera started to follow her and then turned back to Jackie. "I'm really sorry about this. I've tried to be fair with her, but there's just something about that woman that I don't trust."

"I know. I'll fix it, I promise."

An hour passed before the telephone in Jackie's office rang. "She's here and headed for your office. Short of throwing my body in front of her, I don't think I could have stopped her. Her face is blood red, and she looks really angry."

"Thanks. Send Joni in."

There was one rap and the door opened before Jackie could say, "Come in." Jackie was standing next to her desk. "Won't you have a seat," she said to Carin.

"No, I won't have a seat. You said you'd take care of things last night. I come in this morning and nothing's changed," she whined.

"Carin, last night I told you to go home and sleep it off —" Jackie stopped when she heard the knock on her door. "Come in." Jackie saw the expression on Carin face when Joni stepped inside the office.

"What's she doing here?"

"I asked her to join us."

"I don't want her here. I want her fired."

"Carin, I'm not going to fire her. Why don't we sit down and talk about this calmly." Joni stepped around Carin and sat down, leaving the chair closest to Jackie's desk for Carin.

"I'm calm. I'm as calm as they get," Carin said through clenched teeth. "I'm so calm I'm ready to pass out, that's how calm I am."

"Look," Jackie held up her hands to stop the onslaught of words. "I think we have a problem here, and I think —"

"You bet there's a problem," Carin interrupted. "You promised me that job. I deserve that job. And I know what's going on here." She looked accusingly at Joni. "Well, I'll tell you this, Miss La-di-da Doctor, there's a problem here and it's going to get bigger 'cause I quit." Carin's scarlet face reminded Jackie of a child holding its breath. "And you haven't heard the last of me." Carin opened the door and stormed out.

Jackie gave Joni a stunned look, and then Joni got up and closed the door. "Jackie, I'm not sure what all those threats were about, but I believe her. I don't think we've heard the last of her."

Vera knocked once and then stepped inside. "She flew past me and nearly knocked down one of our patients," she said to Jackie.

Jackie frowned. "I think once she calms down she'll be all right. I'll call Darrel tomorrow and see if he can tell us what's going on."

"I wouldn't do that if I were you," Joni said. "Right now he's going to believe his wife, and I don't think there's anything you can say that will change that," Joni insisted.

"I agree with Joni. Calling Darrel is just a waste of time. He's as numb as they come," Vera said. "Did you fire her?"

"No, she quit." Jackie turned to Joni. "You heard her say that she quit. I didn't fire her. I can't see what she can possibly do. I expect she'll demand her vacation pay. She's been here enough months to qualify. Other than that, I think there's nothing to worry about, really."

"Frankly I'm glad she's gone," Vera huffed. "These past few weeks haven't been very pleasant, but if it were up to me I wouldn't give her any money. But I expect the law requires it."

"Whether the law requires it or not, it's the right thing to do," Jackie said. "Now can we get back to work? I wouldn't be surprised but that this little storm of hers will be all over town by late this afternoon. I think what we need to do is get back to the business we do well and forget about her."

"Okay." Joni got up and stood next to Vera at the door. "But promise me you won't call Darrel. I don't think that would be a good idea right now."

"I promise."

"I could hear her yelling clear out in the office," Vera said to Joni as they walked down the hall. "Thank goodness it was the lunch hour and there were just a few patients in the lobby."

"I'm glad for that," Joni said.

"You're worried."

"Yes, I am. I think there's more going on here than we realize."

"What do you mean?"

"I don't know." Joni stopped at the first examining room. "But I think Carin's reaction or overreaction was way out of proportion to my being made senior nurse."

"You don't think she'd try to hurt Jackie or you?"

"No, not physically. But who knows what Darrel might do."

"You're right. You know, I think I just might ask the sheriff to have his deputies keep an eye on the place when they drive by. Wouldn't hurt if they stopped in occasionally to say hi."

"Would they do that?"

"They'd better, he's my first cousin," Vera said with a laugh. "His mother and my mother were sisters. I used to knock him down, sit on him, and pour dirt in his face. Used to try and aim for his mouth. He sure could holler."

Joni gave an exultant laugh. She somehow found it hard to believe that this matronly woman with the steel gray hair would wrestle anyone to the ground. "Why'd you do that?"

"'Cause he used to tease me. Called me names and I'd

whup him. He got a lot of dirt in his face that summer. Stopped teasing me after that," Vera sniffed. "'Course I was bigger than him, and his daddy said he'd beat him if he ever hit a woman. So I had a real advantage there," she added.

"Remind me to never make you angry," Joni teased.

"I haven't thought about that in years. Well" — she patted Joni on the shoulder — "Guess I'd better go call my cousin. And let's get the rest of the patients in the examining rooms. I'll send them back."

The next three weeks passed quickly. Jackie was looking forward to Sondra's arrival. Vera had hired a carpenter, and the storage room was converted into an office for Sondra. Sondra and Jamie were moving this very weekend, and Jackie had volunteered to help them unpack. Even the pain over Dana's departure was starting to subside. Dana hadn't called since Carin had interrupted their telephone call, and Jackie found that she was actually relieved. She continued to resist the temptation to call her. Each time they had talked, the conversation ended with Jackie either mad or sad. She and Joni had fallen into a comfortable rhythm at the office. She had suggested to Vera that they hire another nurse, but her office manager had vetoed the idea until after Sondra was on staff.

Jackie hummed as she walked toward her office. Just two more hours, then hospital rounds, and she'd have the entire weekend off. God, she thought, she hadn't felt this relaxed in months.

"Jackie?" she turned around to see Vera walking toward her carrying a letter. "Could I see you a minute, privately?"

"Sure, Vera, come in." Jackie stepped aside for her office manager. She noticed the chalky pallor of Vera's face as she walked past her. "What's up?"

"This." Vera handed her the letter.

"Dear Dr. Claymont," Jackie read out loud. Jackie looked up at the letterhead. "This is from the Maine Human Rights Commission." She sat down at her desk as she read. She looked up at Vera. "Carin has filed a sexual harassment claim against me. It says here she had a hundred and eighty days to file a claim. They've set a fact-finding conference for next month in Augusta. Did you read this?" she said to Vera. "If reasonable grounds for this complaint are found, both parties will try to reach a voluntary agreement. If a voluntary agreement cannot be reached, the case will be referred to the Commission Council with a request for litigation," she read. She threw the letter on her desk. "I don't believe this. Litigation. I don't understand. Vera, I never touched that woman, never even thought about touching her."

"I know. This is piled high and deep." Jackie could see the color returning to Vera's face.

"Is Joni here?"

"She left about ten minutes ago. Do you want me to call her?"

"No, I will." Jackie tugged at her eyebrow. "In my years as a doctor —" She stopped. "My god, can you imagine the publicity this will generate? Local woman doctor preys on nurse. I think I'm going to be sick." She ran her hands through her hair.

"First off, no one's going to believe this for a minute."

"Don't kid yourself, Vera. I'm gay, and there are people who think all gay people are sexual predators. Do you realize how many Baptist and Pentecostal patients I'm going to lose? We are the only clinic in town. Before, my being gay didn't matter because it wasn't out there for everyone to examine. But this is different, this is small-town America, and once this becomes an issue, I'm not only going to lose patients but am going to be preached about from the pulpit. And my reputation . . . well, it's forever going to be tainted. I've got to stop this." Jackie jumped up and then sat down again. She impulsively picked up the telephone and dialed. "Hi, Kristan. Good, I'm glad you're there. You and Jennifer going to be home tonight? I'd like to come over. I need some advice." Jackie listened. "No, I'd rather not talk about it on the telephone. Skip supper, really. I just want to talk with you two." She looked up at the clock. "Good, I have rounds to make, and then I'll be there. And Kristan, chill a big bottle of wine. We're going to need it."

"Is that a good idea?"

"Jennifer's an attorney, albeit a district attorney, but she can at least give me some advice," Jackie said. She picked up the letter again and reread it. "I don't believe this." She held it out to Vera. "Vera, you know this isn't true."

"I do. And I'll tell you what I'd like to do. If that woman walked into this office this moment, I'd first rip out all that brown hair she constantly keeps patting and then I'd roll her on the ground and dump dirt in her mouth. 'Cause that's what she's spewing. No, dear, I don't believe it, but I'm worried."

"Me too, my friend. Me too. I should call Joni immediately."

"If you don't, I will."

Jackie looked helplessly at her office manager. "I don't have the number."

"I do," Vera said as she picked up the telephone. "Here," she handed the receiver to Jackie.

"It's ringing. And ringing some more. Ah, Joni, hi, this is Jackie. I'd appreciate it if you'd call me at the office as soon as you come in. I'll be here another half-hour. After that you can page me at the hospital."

Jackie picked up the letter again. "I can't believe this." Jackie sighed. "You want to say I told you so?" she said, remembering Vera's distrust of the woman.

"No, I don't," Vera's voice was purposeful. "That woman surprised even me. She has the instincts of a poisonous snake, and I think she's been slithering around this for a long time." Vera pointed at the letter in Jackie's hand. "I don't think this just happened."

Jackie had difficulty focusing on her duties at the hospital. Joni had called, and Jackie had asked her to meet her at Kristan and Jennifer's house. After giving her nurse directions, Jackie finished her rounds and went to their house.

Kristan stepped outside as soon as Jackie drove up. "This must be pretty bad. Joni's already here. God, Jackie, what's going on?"

"Get me a glass of wine and I'll tell you." She smiled at Joni, who was standing next to Jennifer in the kitchen. Jennifer walked over and gave her a hug.

"I don't know what this is about, but we're here for you," Joni said quietly. Jackie could feel her strength and felt better.

"I know."

"Let's sit in the living room," Jennifer suggested.

Kristan tucked a bottle of wine under her arm and picked up a tray of glasses.

"Let me help you." Joni reached for the tray.

"You want to tell us what's going on?" Kristan said as she popped the cork on the bottle.

Jackie pulled the letter out of her black bag and handed it to Jennifer. "Go ahead, read it out loud," Jackie said. Neither Joni or Kristan said anything as Jennifer read, but Jackie watched as the expressions on her friends' faces changed from mild interest to incredulity.

"Wow," Joni said quietly.

"The bitch," Kristan said. "Jennifer, what are Jackie's options?"

Jennifer leaned back on the couch. "This is a tough one, Jacks."

"Tell me about it."

"This was a major topic last month at our annual convention. It's the he-said/she-said of Clarence Thomas and Anita Hill. I think the moderator said something like ninety percent of all women nationwide have experienced some form of sexual harassment in the workplace. And sexual harassment isn't just restricted to men and women. There have been incidences where men have been sexually harassed by female supervisors and even some cases where a gay or lesbian has won in some same-sex cases. In Maine, the state requires all companies that employ fifteen or more employees to offer some kind of training for staff about sexual harassment. This is a very serious charge."

"And that's all it is. I never touched the woman."

"Sexual harassment isn't just restricted to unwelcome sexual advances. There're suggestive or lewd remarks, unwanted hugs, touches, kisses, a request for sexual favors in return for a promotion."

Jackie stood up and began to pace. "None of those things happened." Jackie's voice belied her frustration.

"Okay if I put my lawyer's hat on?"

"That's why I'm here."

"Have you two ever been alone?"

"A few times." Jackie gave Jennifer a puzzled frown. "But not for any length of time. She invited me over to her house shortly after she started working at the clinic. It was one of those invitations you get where you're put on the spot and don't know how to wiggle out of it. Darrel was in the living room watching a baseball game, and we had dinner in the kitchen. I got out of there as fast as I could, in fact, mostly because I was bored to tears." She stopped and looked at Joni. "We met at the hospital. Your Aunt Ceila had had a mild heart attack."

"Right," Joni agreed.

"If I remember" — she gestured at Joni — "we had coffee at my house later."

"Yes, we did."

Jackie felt a jolt of excitement. "Nothing happened. Joni and I spent the rest of the evening talking at my house."

"Have there been other times?"

"She has come into my office at the clinic, but only for a few minutes. She'd ask some mundane question or chatter about what she and Darrel had planned for that night, but that was it."

"Any witnesses?"

"No."

"Was the door opened or closed?"

Jackie frowned as she tried to recall those instances. "Both, I guess. I never thought about it."

"Any other times?" Jennifer probed.

"The night before she quit, she was at my house, a little blitzed or maybe trying to appear blitzed. That was the night you showed up, remember?"

"Yes, I do. How long had she been there before I got there?" Jennifer asked.

"Five, maybe ten minutes, not long."

"But you were alone."

"Oh yeah, we were alone."

"What did she want?

"She wanted me to reprimand Vera and fire Joni. I thought she'd calmed down, but the next day she stormed into my office and yelled that she was going to quit. Said I had lied to her about firing Joni. It was a real scene." Jackie looked helplessly at Joni.

"What about you, Joni. She ever say anything to you about Jackie?"

Joni rubbed her forehead. "It's hard to remember. Carin's the kind of woman you only half listen to. She was always talking about herself or about Darrel. She knew Jackie was gay, or at least thought she was. I remember that every time Dana was in the office, she talked a lot about her."

"Talked about her how?"

"Her looks, her career. She seemed fixated on it. It was strange." Joni stopped and looked cautiously at Jackie.

"Go on," Jennifer said.

"She seemed to be comparing herself to Dana. I saw Dana the few times she stopped at the clinic to pick Jackie up. She's a very beautiful woman. Jackie and I discussed this before . . ." Joni looked at Jackie. "I think Carin in some weird way felt she was in competition with her. It always made me uncomfortable. After I was made senior nurse, I stopped having lunch with her. I felt a book was better than listening to her."

"Jackie ever come on to you?"

"What are you saying?" Jackie yelled. "What do you think I am, some kind of predator?"

Jennifer smiled. "No, I don't think anything of the sort, but, Jackie, these are the kinds of questions the Human Rights investigator will ask. You realize," Jennifer said to Joni, "you'll be called to testify. She'll probably try to pull you into the middle of this, claim that you got the job in exchange for sexual favors, something she refused to give."

Jackie sat forward in her chair. "Nothing happened."

Jennifer held up her hand to quiet her friend. "I know," she said gently, "but there are essentially two categories that the courts or the Maine Human Rights Commission look at. The first is easy. It's called *quid pro quo*. Translated, it means put out or get out, sleep with me if you want to get a promotion. The second is the intolerable workplace environment, a more difficult area but one the courts have upheld. And that's simply that Carin refused to sleep with you and that Joni did, so Joni got the promotion."

"I wouldn't do that. Jackie wouldn't do that," Joni said, emphasizing each word.

"Have you two ever been alone?"

"Yes, many times. We've had dinner together several times in the past few months," Jackie answered.

"At restaurants or at your houses?"

"All of the above," Joni said miserably.

"Any witnesses?"

"Bob," Jackie said, "but somehow I have a feeling you're going to say she doesn't count."

"Unfortunately not."

Jennifer scratched her ear as she reread the letter. "Did you do a background check on this woman before you hired her? Check her references, things like that?"

"I called the hospital where she'd left. They confirmed she'd been an employee there and for how long. You know how closed mouth these places are, afraid they might be sued if they say too much."

"Where was she last employed?"

"A hospital in Atlanta."

"You have any friends down there?"

"Not really, but I could call some of my medical colleagues, see if they have any former classmates working there. Why?"

"This could be a pattern. It'd be nice to demonstrate that when she doesn't get her own way she screams sexual harassment. And I think you should call your attorney. Who is it?"

"Rebecca Sterling."

"I don't imagine she's handled a lot of cases like this. We don't have the numbers they have in the rest of the country. She should recommend someone. Maybe an attorney in Bangor or Portland."

"What about that person you said was handling your seminar. Could he recommend someone?" Kristan asked.

"She, and that's a very good idea, I'll call her Monday."

"I know this probably sounds petty, but this won't get in the newspapers will it?"

Kristan stared at her wineglass. "Unfortunately, it could."

"Oh god. Can't you do something? You're my friend, for crissakes."

"Jackie, what are you asking me to do? Every couple of months the Maine Human Rights Commission sends us a list of cases that are going to go before the full Board of Commissioners for approval. They are cases that an investigator has said either aye or nay to as far as harassment in the work place is concerned. Most of the cases never get into the newspaper because they are Mary Smith claiming that Joe Blow at some small, nondescript factory in Saco did a touchy-feely on her. Other cases do get into the newspaper. I've written several stories about former employees claiming their bosses sexually harassed them. Generally, it depends on how egregious the case is. I wrote one such story years ago about a business owner in Mill Town who not only wanted a woman employee to sleep with him, he also wanted her to sleep with one of his other male employees. That's what I mean by *egregious*."

"Nothing egregious happened between Carin and me." Jackie could feel her anger rising.

"I know that," Kristan said in a calm voice. "But you don't know what she's going to allege in her complaint."

"Whatever she alleges will be a damn lie. You'd put lies about me in your newspaper?" Jackie could feel her voice rise even though she was trying to control her emotions.

Kristan rubbed the palm of her hand against her forehead. Jackie watched as Jennifer reached out and touched the back of Kristan's neck. Kristan gave Jennifer a grateful smile. "First of all, I won't be writing about you. You're my best friend and there would definitely be a conflict of interest. But it will be written about because of the nature of the case. We don't have that many same-sex harassment cases in Maine, and this is one of those instances where an editor is going to feel that the facts of the case and the people involved warrant a news story. And you know what, that editor would be making the right call."

"I don't believe this. We've been friends since we were in first grade, and you'd agree to publish this kind of —"

"Can I interrupt here?" Jennifer's tone demanded attention. "Jackie, I think you need to get a handle on this. The enemy is not Kristan. Let's stay focused. Joni, is there any reason to believe that Carin might try to enlist you as an ally in this?"

"I don't think so. If anything, I think she'd see me as the enemy."

"Why's that?"

"I was hired after her. After Jackie and Vera promoted me, that's all I heard from her. Most of the time they were snide remarks. I mostly ignored them."

"What kinds of snide remarks?"

"Things like, who'd I have to sleep with to get the promotion. I just ignored her."

Jennifer shook her head. "I think this little lady has been building a case against you for some time," she said to Jackie. "Look, my friend, your only hope is to delve into her past, find out if she's filed similar cases in other states. The medical community should be able to help you there because they should know if she's ever filed or threatened to file a similar case.

"An attorney won't have as much success finding that out, especially if she filed a claim and it didn't go anywhere. It only becomes public record if an investigator rules on the facts. Even if he finds against her, it's still public record. For a buck a page you can request a copy of any state Human Rights Commission report. So what you need to do is give the investigator enough evidence to challenge her credibility. That information needs to be in his hands before he starts the fact-finding part of the investigation. Right now she's claiming sexual harassment. You have to prove that she has done the same thing in other jobs. By the way, where's she from?"

"Atlanta," Jackie and Joni said together. The double response seemed to break the tension, and Jackie and Joni laughed.

"God knows she told us enough times," Joni said. "It was, in Atlanta we did this, or my momma and daddy just l-o-v-e Atlanta, they couldn't understand how I could leave. You get the picture."

"What a mess." Jackie groaned.

"I'm not going to pretend it isn't," Jennifer said quietly. "But we can either sit here and complain about what a mess this is, or we can mobilize and discredit this woman. Monday, I'll call the attorney who served as the moderator for that sexual harassment seminar I was at and see if she can recommend a good attorney. Jackie, you need to get in touch with colleagues, past and present, and find out if they have any contacts in Atlanta. Look at her résumé. She would certainly have provided you with one. Start naming off places she worked and see if anyone knows someone there."

"What can I do?" Joni asked.

"You have contacts through your nursing associations. Call them to find out if anyone knew her from before. It's painstaking work, but it could make a difference in where this case goes."

"I hate to be the cynic in this," Kristan said. "But what if her only motivation is money?"

"I don't understand," Jackie said.

"I hadn't thought about that." Jennifer chewed on her bottom lip. "But it's a good question. That could be what this is all about."

"What do you mean *money*?" Jackie said again.

"What if she and, what's her husband's name?"

"Darrel," Joni answered.

"What if she and Darrel showed up at your office and said

they'd drop the charge in exchange for, say, ten thousand or a hundred thousand?"

"My god, that's blackmail."

"Wouldn't be the first time," Jennifer said quietly. "The motivation could be money. Nothing would surprise me."

"I'd say, no. A huge, in-your-face no." Jackie raised her voice for emphasis.

"Even though it could mean keeping this quiet?" Kristan persisted. "No publicity, a quiet payoff. No one would know."

"If you're suggesting I'd pay blackmail, you don't know me very well."

Joni could hear the hurt in Jackie's voice. "I don't think Kristan is suggesting that." Joni cleared her throat. "I think she's saying that you have to be prepared because that could be what's driving this. Frankly, I think Kristan is right. Carin and Darrel could have plotted this together. The times I did listen to her, money was an important part of her conversation. She obsessed over it. Someday, she said, she would live on the ocean. She complained a lot that it had cost them their savings for Darrel to start his plumbing and heating business. I don't think Kristan is that far off the mark."

"What should I do?"

"Jennifer certainly wouldn't suggest this, but I will," Kristan said. "This state allows telephone conversations or any conversation for that matter to be recorded as long as one party knows that a recording device is being used. I think if she's stupid enough to try to blackmail you, then by golly you should get her on tape. That would be your best evidence against her."

"Note, that's the reporter talking, not the attorney." Jennifer glanced at Kristan. "Before you tape anyone, I suggest you discuss it with your attorney. She may disagree or suggest any request for money be handled through her."

Jackie closed her eyes and listened as the grandfather clock in Kristan's living room struck midnight. "God, I'm tired." She held up her wineglass. "I came here to drink enough to drive the pain away, and I haven't even touched my glass."

"Would you like to stay here tonight?" Jennifer asked.

"Thank you, that's really sweet, but" — she got up — "my God, I've forgotten Bob."

"Where is she?" Joni asked.

"At the day-care center. I've been so preoccupied with my own problems, I forgot to call Kathy and tell her I wouldn't pick her up until later. Should I call her now?" Jackie looked anxiously at the clock again.

"Bad idea, friend," Kristan said. "I doubt Kathy has been sitting near the telephone waiting for your call. She probably figures you got hung up in some medical emergency and will pick up Bob tomorrow."

"Oh wow, this is our first night apart."

"Jackie, for gosh sakes, will you get a grip? This is an eight-month-old dog you're talking about. She won't remember five minutes after you pick her up that you forgot her."

Jackie noticed the teasing tug of Kristan's mouth and put her head back and laughed. "Come here." She held out her arms, and Kristan walked over. The two women hugged. "You're right, my friend. I'm going home," she announced. "I'm exhausted. You guys look beat, and, Joni, you look as tired as I feel. Let's all go home."

Jennifer walked over and hugged Jackie. "This is going to turn out all right. You've got a heck of a team here."

"I know." Jackie could feel tears stinging at the edges of her eyes. "Don't forget Vera. She's on our side too."

"How'd she take it?" Kristan asked.

"Aside from threatening to pummel the woman to death, she was really quite calm about it. I suspect that she's been chewing on this all night and that I'll hear from her tomorrow. Good night, you guys, and thanks." Jackie hugged Kristan and then Jennifer again.

She held the door open for Joni and they walked out together.

"Jackie, if there's anything I can do to help you, you know I will," Joni said softly.

"I know." Jackie looked up. "Look at all those stars. Somehow this all seems so insignificant when you compare it to that. A September sky, clear and full of a million stars."

"Yes, but murderously maddening," Joni said, following Jackie's gaze. She reached out and touched Jackie's arm. "Would you like me to give you a ride home? You look exhausted."

"I'm fine." Jackie walked Joni to her car. "Really, I'm fine." They stood awkwardly by the car. "I'd hug you, but I'm afraid people will think it's some form of sexual harassment."

Joni shook her head and chuckled. "I can give you a hug. In fact, I think you need one." She put her arms around Jackie's neck and held her close.

Jackie stumbled as she stepped back.

There was an embarrassed silence while they each waited for the other to say something. Finally Joni said, "Good night." Joni opened the door to her car and watched as Jackie started toward her own. "Do me a favor."

"Sure," Jackie said wearily.

"This is going to be a long weekend for you. Call me if you need to talk. Don't try to tough this out alone. I know how disconcerting that can be."

"I will, I promise."

Chapter 14

White arrows of lightning — like the ones she had felt when she had hugged Jackie — were all she could think about Saturday morning. Hugging Jackie had felt unequivocally seductive, and she hadn't wanted to stop. She'd wanted to pull Jackie hard against her, taste her lips, run her hands all over her body. Joni shivered as she stepped out of the hot shower.

She threw on her running suit and went into her kitchen. She dumped coffee beans into the grinder and felt comfort in the mindless act of grinding them. She poured the beans into the filter, added water to the pot, and snapped it on. She walked over to the window and looked out at the ocean.

Something happened last night, and she needed to assign some kind of order to it in her mind. She watched a robin hopping around in her back yard in pursuit of worms, and for the first time, she could relate. She felt just as fragile as the bird. Jackie had looked to her for comfort and nothing else.

After Alex died, she had wanted to escape everything that reminded her of their life together, including the touch of another woman's hand. Now her body was ablaze wanting Jackie to touch her. This is stupid, she chided herself. The woman is in the middle of a major disaster, and I want to make love to her.

What had Jennifer called it? Workplace environment? If an investigator asked her had she slept with Jackie to get the promotion, she would be able to answer truthfully that she hadn't. But what if? She remembered another time and another woman who had faced a similar situation. Joni shivered; she refused to allow her mind to go there.

Joni turned back to the coffeepot. She poured herself a cup of the Colombian brew before she walked out onto her patio. She leaned her face back to suck in the last of the declining summer sun. What if the investigator asked her if she had any feelings for Jackie? Then what? What would she say? I hugged my boss out of sympathy one night when she was truly hurting because this bitch is making her life hell, and I found out that I wanted to immediately scale a mountain with her. Take her in my arms and crush her naked body against mine. That I wouldn't stop there, I would make love to her the entire night. That I wanted to make her cry from pleasure and not pain. Joni quaked at the thought.

She stood up and rubbed the back of her neck. That, she thought, would pretty well affirm any claim Carin had against Jackie. Joni ignored the first four rings of the telephone. She walked over to her screen and listened as her answering machine kicked on. "Hi Joni, it's Jackie." As Joni rushed to open the screen, she spilled hot coffee on her leg.

"I'm here, don't hang up."

"Good morning."

"Good morning to you," Joni said quietly as she reached for a towel to wipe the coffee off her running pants.

"Have I interrupted something?"

"No, I just spilled some coffee. Nothing serious," Joni said as she vigorously swiped her leg. Her skin tingled from the heat. "I hope you slept well."

"I slept, but not well. Look, I feel silly, but I really don't want to be alone today. I'd like to go for a walk. Anyway, did you mean it when you said you'd . . ."

"Of course." Joni could hear the uncertainty in Jackie's voice.

"I could call Kristan, but, well, she has her own problems right now."

"I'd be happy to spend the day with you. How about lunch somewhere and maybe a walk on the beach? Or we could go to the refuge. Watch the birds. Maybe see a moose."

"I'd like that. I'll make up some sandwiches."

"Don't, please. Let me take care of that. Why don't we meet say" — Joni looked at the clock — "at ten?"

"That'd be great. Do you want to come here or should I pick you up at your house?"

"I'll pick you up."

"See you then. And, Joni, thanks."

Joni hung up the telephone and opened her refrigerator door. She pulled open the meat tray and found some ham. It had a green iridescent glow to it. "Good, I can give her food poisoning. That sure would take her mind off her problems," she groused out loud. She dumped the ham in the trash and started pulling open cupboards. She had less than fifty minutes to figure out lunch, get dressed, and pick up Jackie. She pulled her wet running pants off and threw them on a chair. There were red splotches on her thigh where she had spilled the coffee. No permanent damage, she thought. Just stupid damage.

She paused in her search for food and smiled. That's what she and Alex used to call all the dumb mistakes people made in life. Like the time Alex turned left in front of a car and narrowly missed causing a serious collision. She said she had been thinking about something else and not really paying attention. That, she had said, would have been stupid damage. After that they would laugh and call all those small errors of life stupid damage.

Joni inhaled. Slow down. Warp speed is not going to help me solve this problem, she said to herself. She opened the door where she kept her canned goods and pulled out a can of tuna. She looked in the crisper and found slightly limp celery and an onion. She soaked the celery in ice-cold water and peeled away the discolored part of the onion. She put two eggs on to boil and then looked in the breadbox. The bread had started to grow hair from the mold. "Good, I'll feed her this, give her her daily dose of penicillin." Joni smiled as she tossed the bread in the garbage on top of the iridescent ham.

She could stop and buy bread. She pulled out her picnic basket and looked inside. At least there was nothing growing in there. She mixed up the tuna salad. She would add the eggs as soon as they cooled. She threw knives and forks and spoons into the picnic basket, along with a fresh roll of paper towels. She could buy bread, chips, and whatever else at the store on her way to pick up Jackie. She put several bottles of sparkling water in her small cooler. Not bad, she thought. The telephone rang just as she finished. Maybe, she thought, Jackie had changed her mind. She picked up the telephone.

"Joni, this is Carin."

Joni could feel her heart decelerate. "Carin, where are you?"

"At home. Darrel had a job this morning, and I thought I'd call you. I realize that I acted like a beast toward you, and

I just called to apologize." Joni felt a small feeling of panic overtake her as Carin seemed to rush her words. "Really, none of this is your fault. I think you just got trapped in the middle of this. Gosh, I think we should just remain friends and not let this come between us. We are friends, aren't we?" she demanded.

"Carin, you're upset." Joni distrusted the calm in Carin's voice. It was part of the woman's deceptively composed demeanor somehow. "Why don't you and Dr. Claymont talk this over?"

"Don't you want to be friends?" she asked sweetly.

Joni knew she had to placate her. "We can only be friends if you stop this nonsense with Dr. Claymont."

Carin's laugh was forced. "No way," she said sharply. "I know what you're trying to do. And it won't work. I know how you feel about that woman," she added angrily. "Things are going to happen. I know you're a lesbian. I was willing to overlook it, but not now," she shouted.

Joni pulled out a chair and sat down. It felt as if her knees wouldn't hold her any longer. She could feel her energy being sucked up by Carin's anger. "Carin" — Joni swallowed — "I think you need to get control of yourself."

"Control? I am in control, sweetie." Carin's voice was calm again. Joni wondered at the roller coaster of emotions. "Won't answer my question. Well, it explains why you got the job over me." Joni could hear the strain in Carin's voice as she struggled to remain in control. "Why, there'd be no other reason except if you were sleeping with the boss, right? Look at you. You're short and frumpy. I admit you have a so-so face, but in a moon sort of way. Why, I'm more like that woman who left her," she hissed in Joni's ear. "Dana, that's who I look like." Joni heard Carin pause as she realized what she was saying. "Not that I'd want to be like her," she added quickly. "The thought of making love with a woman is loathsome and revolting. It says in the Bible you shouldn't sleep with your own kind."

"Carin, where are you going with this? You know I haven't slept with Jackie, and you know she isn't interested in either of us. She's been nothing but professional at the office. Why —"

"I'm not going to talk about anything else. Now are you a queer or not?" she demanded.

"Carin, you're right. I'm not going to talk about anything else either. Please don't call me anymore," Joni said as she hung up the telephone.

Joni's nerves were humming. Carin reminded her of a game that she and her friends used to play as a child. They'd all go over to Mr. Clark's pasture and play with the electrical fence. You'd grab hold of the hot wire and then touch the other kids on the nose with the tip of your finger. You could feel the tingle of the low-voltage electricity coursing through your body, but you didn't feel the shock until you touched their nose. That's what Carin reminded her of, a hot wire that was sending off all these life jolts.

Joni reached for the telephone to call Jackie but then put it down. She went into the bedroom, put on jeans, a flannel shirt, and hiking boots. She picked up the picnic basket, tossed the still warm eggs inside, and went to her car.

Jackie was waiting outside for her as she drove up. Bob was romping around her feet. She had a small bag in her hand. She opened the back door and Bob scrambled into the seat. "Good morning," Jackie said as she climbed in the car. "You look as though you got as much sleep as I did."

Joni's expression was teasing. "Thank you, Doctor, and I'd love to pay you the same compliment. You look as terrible as I feel."

Jackie laughed. "Good. We've gotten that out of the way. Now we can look forward to our walk at the refuge unencumbered by life's truths."

"Exactly. Seriously, how did you sleep last night?" Joni asked.

"Not well, I kept waking up angry. I realized that wasn't productive and wasn't going to help me get back to sleep. I got up around four and just sat looking out at the ocean. At some point I fell asleep in my chair. I woke up this morning and decided that I would rather not be alone. So I called you."

"I'm glad." Joni chewed on the inside of her cheek. She wondered when she should bring up Carin's telephone call.

Jackie looked back at the picnic basket and the brown paper bag that Bob was trying to climb inside. She reached back and pulled the dog's head away from the bread. "Are we going to be picnicking a long time?" she asked as she eyed the groceries.

Joni laughed. "No, I found this morning that I had few things to offer by way of a picnic, so I stopped at the store. I hope you like tuna?"

"Maine's staple. Yes, I do. I find, however, that everyone has their own recipe for tuna or potato salad. I know about your nursing skills. This will give me an opportunity to judge your tuna skills."

"Don't be too critical. Except for tuna, mayonnaise, onion, and eggs, I had little else to offer. Oh, and rather limp celery that I iced."

"Sounds perfect."

Jackie had been watching her as they talked, and Joni could feel rippling heat coursing through her body. Her cheeks felt warm. Stop it, Joni said to herself. She looked at Jackie, who had turned to watch the scenery. She liked her profile. Her chin was strong. She knew Jackie was in her fifties, but she had no bottom bulge or over-forties sag that was so much a part of an aging chin.

She also liked the way Jackie looked her in the eyes when she talked. She wondered if it was something Jackie had learned in medical school or if it was how she'd always related to people. She remembered Dr. Schultz's telling her that patients will not trust you if you cannot look them in the eye, especially when you have bad news. You must look them in the eye, even if they do not look back, he had said.

"What are you thinking about?" Jackie turned back to her.

"Dr. Schultz." Joni laughed.

"Dr. Schultz. Well, I didn't expect that answer. Who is Dr. Schultz?"

Joni then related why she had thought of him.

"Gosh," Jackie laughed. "That must be taught in every medical school. For me it was Dr. Steven Pottle. A wizened man with this big voice. He used to demand that we look him in the eye whether we were asking a question or talking to him after class about our grade. In fact, I often thought that the line between an *A* and a *B* was how well I looked him in the eye."

"Strange, the avenues our brain takes once that portion is awakened by some word or phrase."

"Yes." Jackie chuckled.

Joni pulled the car into the parking lot at the Moosehorn refuge. She was pleased to see that they were alone. The bikers, power hikers, and birders had not yet stirred. "Eat or walk?"

"Let's walk. It's been ages since I've walked out here." Jackie opened the door for Bob, who immediately ran over to the grass and began sniffing.

"I come out here a lot. I especially enjoy the spring of the year and watching the woodcock." Joni inhaled deeply.

"Ah, the timberdoddle. I haven't seen them in years."

Joni relaxed, enjoying the pleasure of their newfound affinity. "I love their mating habits. I came out this spring for a tour. At dusk the males sit cheeping in the brush, calling to the females. Then all of a sudden he shoots into the air and does all these aerial acrobats. I guess the better the mating dance, the more attractive he is. I suspect he's looking down to see if she's watching. If the female likes the performance they mate."

"Wouldn't it be fun if our mating habits were that simple."

"And think about how uncomplicated," Joni replied.

They walked the three-mile track on the headquarters road. With each turn, Joni thought about mentioning the telephone call from Carin, but Jackie seemed so relaxed that she hated to ruin their walk. So they talked about everything but the clinic and Carin.

Joni asked about Marianne. "I hope I'm not being insensitive, but does the pain ever go away?"

"It lessens, but never leaves. Since this has happened, I've thought a lot about her. Don't get me wrong, but you remind me a lot of her. That same kind of steady personality."

Joni's spirits plummeted.

"You're awfully quiet."

"I think I would have liked Marianne."

"You would have. She was a nurse like you."

"How'd you meet?"

"I was a first-year resident, and we were at the same hospital. I wish I could say it was love at first sight, but that wouldn't be accurate. We spent a lot of nights in the emergency room, as you do. Slow nights you sit and talk a lot; busy nights you pour out every ounce of energy you have. Anyway, one night she invited me to dinner, and I think essentially seduced me. Not to say I hadn't had other experiences. But they were the closet gropes of youth. She was the first woman I'd ever lived with." Joni could hear the sadness in Jackie's voice. "We were together ten years. Then she found the lump. It had already spread to her lymph nodes. Anyway . . ."

"And Dana?"

"We met in an ice storm."

"Ice storm?"

Jackie recounted the winter that an ice storm had paralyzed much of Maine. There had been a knock at her door. Dana was standing there, ice hanging from her coat and her hood. She had reminded Jackie of a statuesque ice sculpture.

Her burning red hair peeking out from the hood. Her telephone was out, and she wanted to know if Jackie still had service. Jackie's cell phone was still working and Dana, who had only been back in Bailey's Cove a few weeks, called her parents to tell them that she and their house, which she was housesitting, were all right.

Dana confessed she'd had a crush on Jackie since fifth grade, and they'd made love that night. For a time Dana was content to live in Bailey's Cove, but when an editor for *Time* magazine called, Jackie had seen the excitement in her eyes. She'd encouraged her to accept, and after that there were more and more assignments.

"I like your friends Kristan and Jennifer."

"They're special. Unfortunately, they weren't at their best last night."

"I don't understand."

Jackie paused. "I don't think it would be a breach of ethics if I told you that they are thinking about having a child and that it has created a bit of tension between them."

"I think that's wonderful." Joni pulled a leaf off the maple tree she walked past and rubbed her fingers over it. "What kind of tension?"

"Jennifer wants a child; Kristan is less sure."

"Ah. That's tension. Funny, I've always wanted a child. But I guess it's not something that will ever happen."

"Why not? More and more single women are doing it."

"True. But I think I would rather share that child with someone I loved. What about you?"

"I've never thought about it. When Marianne and I were together, single women and lesbian couples really weren't doing that. I don't think we ever talked about it. Or if we did it was kind of a wish-list kind of thing. I adore children. And with Dana, it really was never an option because she was gone more than she was home, and, well, it just never came up."

"I think you'd be a wonderful mother. I see how kids, regardless of age, relate to you, and . . ." Joni paused. "I think you'd be terrific with your own."

Jackie scratched her ear. "You say you'd like a child, but it can't happen. Why not?"

"I don't see myself in a relationship ever again."

Jackie stopped and looked directly at Joni. "I hope you don't mean that. You're a loving woman. I see how you interact with the children at the office. You'd be a terrific mother. I don't know what happened in the past that makes you say you'd never be in a relationship again, but I hope you're wrong." Jackie turned away and started walking slowly along the path.

"Thank you." Joni said softly. "I think . . ." she stopped. "We're at the headquarters road," she said, more to change the subject.

"Wow, we've walked three miles. I seem to talk a lot when I'm with you. Look, did I say something wrong back there?"

"No, honest." Joni pointed to the picnic tables in front of them. "Would you like to eat or walk some more? There's another trail."

Jackie laughed. "Why don't we sit? I'm sorry. I'm not usually this garrulous and insensitive."

"It's okay. I enjoy listening to you. What you said made me think about what I would want. I would love to have a baby. But I would want to share her with the person I loved, and right now that isn't going to happen." Joni spread the impromptu picnic before Jackie and made each of them a sandwich. Jackie opened the small bag she had with her and poured water and dog food into the bowls. Bob couldn't decide which she wanted first and alternated between eating and lapping water.

"This is very good," Jackie said as she bit into the tuna sandwich.

Joni toyed with one of the potato chips on her plate. She picked it up and then set it down. "Jackie, Carin called me this morning." Joni watched as Jackie set her sandwich down.

"And?"

"She came across friendly at first, but she's seething."

"What did she want?"

Joni hesitated. "She asked me if I was a lesbian. Said it was something that had been bothering her for some time." Joni set her own sandwich down. Somehow she didn't feel very hungry.

"What did you tell her?"

"Nothing. I told her that she needed to speak with you. That's when she turned nasty and I quietly hung up on her."

Jackie sat stroking her chin, something Joni had noticed she did at the clinic when she resorted to her analytical mode. "Are you a lesbian?" Jackie said after a time.

"Yes," Joni said wearily. "In the past it wasn't something I shied away from, but somehow Carin's mind has twisted all of this," Joni hesitated. "I feel that our lives are steadily shifting like tectonic plates slipping under the earth and we don't know where the next fissure will cause a cataclysmic earthquake. That's what Carin is doing. She is manipulating those plates, keeping us on edge. The call this morning was calculated to upset me. She knew I would talk to you about it. It's her way of controlling the situation. I agree with Jennifer, *we* need to take control of this. First, you need a good attorney. And second, we need more information about this woman. I've thought about this all night. I'm going to call a few friends that I went to nursing school with. They'll be shocked to hear from me, but one of them might know someone in the medical community in Atlanta."

"I've already made some calls. I decided last night that I wasn't going to underestimate this woman, and now I think she's confirmed it. She's going for something bigger than two weeks' vacation or unemployment benefits. She wants to embarrass me."

"Something else I thought about. When we used to have lunch together it was clear that Darrel's family doesn't like her. Do you think they might help you?"

"I don't know. I'll talk to Vera about that. She knows everyone or knows someone who knows everyone. I'll get her to get the talking drums started."

"Talking drums?"

"The gossip pipeline. She knows someone who will know someone who will have a story about Darrel and Carin. It's a start."

"What a mess. Jackie, I'll do anything to help you. I just hope my being gay isn't going to make it worse for you. I kept thinking about what Jennifer said last night about workplace environment. I bet she's going to claim I slept with you and that's why I got the promotion."

"She can claim that. But what she doesn't know is that the move to promote you came from Vera. She brought the idea to me. I frankly don't pay all that much attention to the day-to-day administrative things going on at the office. Unless you slept with Vera, I think that argument is going to fail."

Joni laughed at the thought of sleeping with Vera. Jackie joined in the laughter.

"Thanks, I needed that laugh," Joni paused. "Unless all of this is just some twisted and maniacal effort on her part to embarrass you. Or to blackmail you," she said.

"Last night I was thinking that paying her off would be so easy that no one would know. But I can't." Joni heard the determination in Jackie's voice.

"I'm glad." Joni selected each word carefully. "Because somehow I don't think that would silence her. It would only affirm the fantasy she's built in her mind. I feel this is all calculated; she acts and we react. I think it's time to stop reacting and take control," Joni reiterated.

"What kind of fantasy?"

Joni turned dark red with embarrassment. "I think she's had fantasies about sleeping with you."

143

"Me? I've never even demonstrated the least bit interest in her. I . . ." Jackie shrugged. "I've done nothing to even suggest that was a possibility."

"I know." Joni experienced a pang of regret. Isn't that what she'd been doing? Creating fantasies? "I think she's created this fantasy of sleeping with you and its grown into a Frankenstein monster in her mind. She's curious about sleeping with you, but averse because you're a woman. So now she's created this whole construct that suggests you and I slept together and that's why she didn't get the job."

Jackie rubbed her fingers against her temples. "How do I fight that?"

"I don't know, but you have to. Otherwise, her lie wins."

"Agreed," Jackie said reluctantly. She looked at Joni. "You hide your gayness well."

"Not hide. I just don't know what to do with it in a new situation. I know there are people who after they say hello tell you they're gay. I admire them, but I've never been able to do that. I've always been a private person, and I rather like that."

"I don't understand."

"How do I explain this?" Joni absently chewed on a potato chip. "When Carin and I were forced to eat lunch together, she'd chatter on and on about her and Darrel. And if I'd evinced the smallest interest I'm sure she would have told me when and how they did it in bed. I'm not interested in that. I really like my privacy. In Boston, Alex and I had a coterie of gay friends, and I found that I spent more time listening to their problems. When Alex and I had a fight, we tended to resolve it ourselves. I don't think either one of us ever took it outside our relationship. I guess that's what I mean."

"Where's Alex?"

Joni looked down at her hands, which she had been twisting in her lap. She spread out her fingers and laid the palms of her hands on the picnic table. "Alex was forty-four when she died of a heart attack. That was more than two years ago."

Jackie reached out and held Joni's hands with hers. "I'm so sorry, this is really not the time for me to be probing into your personal life. Kristan and Jennifer asked me if you were gay. I've been so focused on my breakup with Dana and this thing with Carin that I never even stopped to think about it."

"There wasn't any need to, but now Carin is going to shift this and twist it into something contorted and insane. Can an investigator ask me if I'm a lesbian?"

"I don't know. But I sure as heck need to find out. I'll call Jennifer as soon as I get home and ask her." Jackie started to gather up the sandwich bags. She looked at her half-eaten sandwich. "I'm sorry" — she pointed at the sandwich — "it really was very good. I'm just not very hungry."

"Don't apologize. Someday this will be behind us and I will cook you the best meal ever. Promise."

Jackie smiled in spite of her distraction. "And I will accept," she said.

Joni drove Jackie back to her house. The entire trip she kept watching out of her rearview and side mirrors, somehow spooked that Carin might be following them. She felt as though the woman was everywhere. And why not, she thought, she wasn't working. All she had to do was plot against Jackie. Joni felt her anger rising again. She pulled into Jackie's driveway and stopped the car.

"Thank you." Jackie got out of the car and reached in the back for Bob. "Believe it or not, for a few hours it really was relaxing."

"For me, too," Joni said softly. She watched as Jackie seemed to want to say something else, but changed her mind.

"See you Monday."

"Yes." Jackie and Bob walked into the house, and Joni sighed. This was madness. They were both protagonists in a mindless play directed by Carin.

Chapter 15

The next few days dragged. Sondra and Jamie had arrived shortly after Labor Day, and some of the day-to-day pressures eased. Jackie had briefed them on Carin's allegation, and Sondra had insisted that Jackie take a few days off, which she refused to do. As when Marianne had died, Jackie found work to be the only constant in her life.

Jennifer had found a female attorney in Portland who had handled Human Rights cases, and Jackie had faxed her a copy of the letter from the Maine Human Rights Commission. The attorney had questioned Jackie, Joni, and Vera on the telephone. Vera was still trying to find one of Darrel's family members who would talk to her about Carin. Now it was a matter of waiting until Carin made the next move.

Although this battle seemed to have rallied her friends around her and even seemed to bring Jennifer and Kristan closer together, Jackie could still see the abyss in her friends' relationship. They had been seeing a counselor, and Jackie was wondering how that was going. Even though the counselor was a friend of hers, it would have been unprofessional for her to discuss their problems even with their doctor.

Jackie was with her last patient of the day when Vera rapped on the examination room door. "When you're finished, Doctor," Vera said. "I'll put this in your office." Vera held up the certified letter.

"Thank you Vera, and ask Joni to join me there too, would you please?" She kept her voice calm and turned back to her patient.

Joni and Vera were waiting for her when she joined them. "Where's Sondra?"

"She left to make hospital rounds. I paged her at the hospital. She wanted to rush right back, but I told her you'd call her at home tonight with the details. No point in all of us being pulled away from what we do," Vera huffed.

Jackie sighed. Vera was feeling the stress along with her. Jackie turned the letter over several times in her hand. "I don't expect this is good news," she said, looking at the return address for the Maine Humans Rights Commission. I wonder if I should call Jennifer and put her on the speaker telephone along with my attorney?"

"I have the numbers right here," Vera said. "Do you want me to do it?"

Jackie turned her telephone around so that Vera could punch in the numbers. Jackie looked at Joni's face. "You look as worried as I feel." She laughed to try to defuse some of her anxiety.

"The hardest part has been this waiting and not knowing what she is going to do," Joni said. "We knew she was going to do something, I was just praying that maybe she'd calm down and realize how stupid this is."

"I was hoping for that, but somehow I knew she would take it to the next step. Funny that we haven't heard from her otherwise. Maybe money isn't the motivation here," Jackie said.

"Maybe."

Vera pushed the last button. "I have Jennifer on line one and Pat Harrington on line two."

"Jennifer, Pat," Jackie said by way of greeting. "I have Vera and Joni here in the office. I thought we might as well open this with everyone listening," Jackie said as she sliced her letter opener through the top. "And the Emmy goes to . . . just kidding," she said when she saw the pain on Joni's face. "There's reference to several statutes here. Let's see . . ." Jackie scanned down the letter. She started to read out loud. " 'Carin Chase, who was employed by your office from February sixth until she left on' blah-blah-blah, 'has filed a claim under Maine's Sexual Harassment in the Workplace, Section 46572 of the Maine Human Rights Act.' Let's see . . ." Jackie read further. " 'Unwelcome sexual advances, requests for sexual favors, and other verbal or physical conduct of a sexual nature constitute sexual harassment when: submission to such conduct is made either explicitly or implicitly a term or condition of an individual's employment; submission to or rejection of such conduct by an individual is used as the basis for employment decisions affecting such individual; or such conduct has the purpose or effect of substantially interfering with an individual's work performance or creating an intimidating, hostile, or offensive working environment.' Wow, that's a mouth full," Jackie said.

"Read me the last paragraph, would you," Pat said over the telephone.

Jackie shuffled through the three pages and started to

read the last paragraph. " 'Mrs. Chase is alleging that on' those dates, I read above," Jackie said to the telephone, " 'Dr. Jackie Claymont, known as the defendant, made threats, demands, or suggestions that her work status was contingent upon her toleration or acquiescence to sexual advances. And that her coworker, Joni Coan, also was subjected to such behavior and was promoted after she acquiesced to that harassment. After which, Carin Chase, known as the plaintiff, quit her job.' She is asking for unspecified damages." Jackie looked at the telephone. "We have sixty days to respond. That's the bottom line."

"Fax me a copy of that, would you?" Pat said.

"Sure, I'll have Vera do it immediately. Jennifer, would you like a copy?"

"No, I don't think you want too many copies of that floating around. Send it to Pat. Pat, I have an idea. I have to go back into court in the next minute. Are you home tonight?"

"Absolutely. Give me a call there."

"Jacks, Kristan and I are with you on this. Anything you need, you call. Promise?"

"Promise."

"Jackie," Pat said after Jennifer had hung up, "don't worry."

"What happens now?"

"I'll request a copy of Carin's statement so we know what she is alleging. I'll take your statements and file our response in the sixty days allotted. Actually, I'll file it the last day. I don't want anyone to think we're too anxious. Then we wait."

"For how long?"

"I have some friends over at the Human Rights Commission; I'll find out how backed up their caseload is. Depending upon that, anywhere from another thirty days to months. If the investigator believes us, the case will go no further. If not, there'll be a hearing in Augusta. We go and Carin goes and he questions her and us."

"Do we get to ask questions?" Jackie asked.

"Absolutely."

"Good. It'll give me a chance to give that woman a piece of my mind," Vera huffed.

Pat laughed. "It's a little more formal than that. Fax that to me so I can review it," she said just before she hung up.

Jackie handed the letter to Vera. "Would you take care of this?"

"Sure. Jackie, I know it's dumb to say don't worry, but you have some really top people handling this."

"I know, Vera. But I think I'll worry just a little bit." Jackie looked affectionately at her longtime friend. Jackie looked at Joni after Vera had left and saw the fear in her face. "Are you okay?"

"Yes." She stood up and turned away from Jackie.

"Whoa, wait a minute." Jackie stopped her at the door. "Are you crying?"

"No," Joni sniffled.

"Come here," Jackie held out her arms.

"I'm sorry." Joni's words were muffled against Jackie's shoulder. "I'm crying because I'm angry. This is so unfair to you. This is just spite, and she's trying to get at you." Joni looked up at Jackie. "She's getting no cooperation from me."

"I know that," Jackie said gently. She took her thumbs and wiped the tears from Joni's cheek. For the first time, Jackie looked deep into Joni's dark brown liquid eyes. She caught her breath and stepped back.

Joni fumbled for a Kleenex on Jackie's desk and wiped her eyes. "I'm sorry. I shouldn't have broken down like that. Really, this isn't what I usually do."

Jackie still was staring at her. "This isn't something either one of us is used to. It's okay," she said.

"I need to tell you something." Joni paused. "Several years before Alex died, we went through a similar incident. Alex was a professor at Boston University. One of her female students came on to her, and when Alex didn't respond, the student claimed that Alex had made sexual remarks, the same stuff

151

Carin's claiming against you. I guess . . ." She choked back a sob. "I guess that's why this has made me so angry. I feel like I'm reliving that same horror. The student demanded money or she'd go to the dean of the college. Alex refused."

"What happened?"

"It was a mess for months. The dean had no choice but to hold an informal hearing. Thank God several of Alex's female students, both past and present, not only stepped forward and testified on her behalf, but also some of them knew the student and actually testified against her. And several of Alex's male colleagues also testified. It seems she'd come on to them also. Anyway" — Joni wiped a fresh Kleenex against her face — "it never got this far, but it accomplished something far more damaging. After that Alex refused to be alone in her office with any student, male or female. She had tenure and gave up her private office for a double unit she could share with another professor. It made her absolutely paranoid. I don't think she ever got over it."

"I can relate to that. I —"

Vera rapped once and opened the door.

"Excuse me." Joni felt embarrassed that Vera had seen her crying. She stepped past the office manager.

"Is she all right?" Vera watched Joni walk down the hall.

"Yes. The stress of this is getting to all of us. Close the door, will you, and sit for a minute. I have to make rounds, but I want to talk to you." Jackie waited until Vera was seated. "I think we should plan for the worst."

"Jackie, don't give up."

"Vera, I'm not. But if our patients hear about this, my practice is going to suffer. You know that and I know that."

"Jackie, I don't think you should made any decisions right now. You're under a lot of stress, and things will look different once this is resolved. This woman is not going to win," Vera insisted.

"She'll win even if she loses." Jackie then told her that

once the Human Rights investigator's report is finished, even if Carin loses, it would be public record and in all the local newspapers."

"Can't Kristan stop that?"

"No," Jackie said sharply and then inhaled. " When I first learned it was something that could go public, I was angry with Kristan, but now I realize it's not her fault. She won't write the story, but it will be written, probably by a reporter in Bangor. You know this community. My female patients will quit, worried I'll touch them inappropriately. Every time I do a gynecological exam you know what they'll be thinking, and their husbands won't want to be touched by me for fear it'll rub off."

"Some will, but I know these people. I've lived here my whole life, well, nearly my whole life." She paused. "I don't think it's going to matter with most people. When you and Marianne first moved back here, people talked. I heard the talk, but then they got to know you and it didn't matter. Now no one even thinks about the fact that you're gay."

Jackie linked her fingers together and studied them. "This is going to make them think about it because this is in their face," Jackie muttered more to herself. "Let's hope my attorney can convince the investigator not to take this to a hearing." She shrugged. "When I first told Jennifer about this, she said it's the he-said/she-said phenomena, but in this instance it's she-said/she-said. It's a matter of which one the investigator believes."

Vera looked at her with pity. "Even if this goes to a hearing," she said matter-of-factly, "you're going to win. You're not thinking of quitting?"

"No, I'd go bonkers. But I do have to think about bringing in a colleague. I have to give my patients a choice. You know some will choose to go elsewhere, and that's not in anyone's best interest. For some my being gay is not going to be something they will feel comfortable with, and the next closest doctor is thirty miles from here. No one should have to travel that far for medical treatment. I think I should start looking now."

"I don't agree. Only a few will leave, a few narrow-minded simpletons who won't remember all the things you did for them. But, Jackie" — Vera scowled at her friend — "don't make any decisions until we know where this is going. Plus, if you make these kinds of decisions now, she wins. She's controlling our lives, and I don't want that bitch to control our lives," she said fiercely. "Let's just wait."

Jackie put her head back and laughed. She had never ever heard Vera refer to anyone as a bitch. "Okay." She held up her hand to stop the onslaught of words. "No lifetime decisions until this is over with," she looked affectionately at her friend. "Would you check on Joni for me?" Jackie relived the jolt she'd felt when she'd wiped the tears from her eyes.

"Sure." Vera started out the door and then turned back. "I feel sorry for her."

"Why? Is something going on I don't know about?"

"She's blaming herself for this. Somehow thinks if she'd befriended the woman, things might have turned out differently."

"That's silly."

"I told her Carin was just spleeny. I had to explain what the word meant to her."

Jackie laughed. "It's not a term used much any more, and certainly not by the medical community. You're right, though. Carin is spleeny."

"I think the term suits her perfectly, and I plan to tell that to the investigator. She's out of sorts, cranky. You call it PMS, but I say she's downright ornery and spleeny. Probably been that way her whole life."

Jackie chuckled as she thought about Vera's characterization. She looked down at her watch. "Got to make rounds. Check on Joni for me, okay?"

"Sure."

Jackie changed out of her lab coat and was picking up her medical bag when Vera opened the door. "She's left. I think you should give her a call this weekend, maybe take her out to dinner. She's carrying a weight on her shoulders."

"I would, but with Sondra here and everything. Would you call her for me?"

Vera frowned. "If you'd like, but I think she'd rather hear from you. She needs to talk about this."

"You handle it, okay?" Jackie kept the bite out of her voice, but she knew Vera could sense her impatience.

"Sure." Vera hesitated at the door. "Have you told Dana?"

"No, and I don't want to."

"How are things between you?"

"Strained. We talk. We're making an effort to be friends. It's amazing how, as you get older, breakups are so civilized. If we both had been twenty years old, there'd have been a lot of screaming and yelling." Jackie stopped. "She asks me how I'm doing, and I tell her everything is peachy-keen. I ask her how things are going and she says wonderful, she's off shooting this or that." Jackie paused as she realized she was using her sarcasm on Vera. "It's better, really. I put away the music we used to listen to. I've stopped thinking about her every minute of the day. Now I only think of her every other minute. She's been like the flu, tough to get over, but after a while, I'll get over it."

"I'm so sorry this happened. I love my niece, but if I could see her right now, I'd give her a swift boot in the you-know-what."

Jackie chuckled. "You're sure sounding like you want to get awfully physical these days. You want to boot your niece and pop Carin. This is a side of you I've never seen before."

"That's because I've never been this mad before. Jackie, anything I can do, you know I would."

"I know, Vera, and I love you for it."

Jackie watched as Vera turned around embarrassed. "Well, I care for you," she grumbled. "I'll go check on Joni."

"Thanks."

After her rounds, Jackie called Sondra and Jamie to see if they wanted to have dinner, but there was no answer. She also called Kristan and Jennifer, but they also were gone. "It's Friday night," Jackie said to Bob. "And nobody's home. Come on, I'll feed you and then we'll take a quick run down on the beach. Good, now I'm talking to my dog out loud." She smiled down at Bob. "Just don't start answering, okay?"

Bob cocked her head as if she understood and danced around Jackie's feet until her food was ready. Several times Jackie looked at the telephone, but put calling Joni out of her mind. Something had happened, and she had felt it and knew Joni had. "She's touched me with her eyes," Jackie said to Bob, who was gobbling her food.

Jackie rubbed her temples with her fingers. "I'm lonely. I'm going through something I've never gone through before, and I'm just lonely," she told herself.

Chapter 16

She'd left the clinic as soon as she'd walked out of Jackie's office. Jackie's touch had turned her knees to water. She had looked into Jackie's eyes, and all she could see was passion, her passion reflected back to her from Jackie. She'd wanted to pull Jackie's mouth against hers, but had resisted. I've fallen in love with her, Joni repeated over and over in her mind on the drive home.

Vera had called her as soon as she had walked in the door and had offered to have dinner with her, but Joni told her she had a migraine and was going to bed.

"What a mess," she said out loud to her kitchen. "What a mess."

Joni knew that Jackie was vulnerable and that the slightest touch would catapult them into bed. But would Jackie later be vexed at what had happened?

My god, Joni sharply rebuked herself. Jackie has just broken up with a woman whom she's been in love with for years. Her career is threatened, and all I can think about is making love to her. Joni shook her head and recalled Jennifer's words about the publicity that would come from this even if Jackie won. Joni's heart ached for Jackie. Anything that would happen between them now would be mindless sex. Joni thought blandly about her choice of words. She could use some mindless sex. "But not now," she said quietly to the air. "Not now."

Joni picked up the telephone on the first ring. "Hello."

"It's me, sweetie," her aunt said.

"Anything wrong?" Joni pulled out a kitchen chair and sat down.

"Not a thing. I'm as fit as a lobster growing a new shell."

"I'm sorry, Auntie." Joni felt a need to explain why she hadn't been in contact with her aunt since she had been hospitalized. "I've been so preoccupied lately with things at work, I neglected to call you."

"Don't you worry about it," her aunt said brightly. "I'm fine, and I didn't have to have anything more done to me. Tests were fine. Blood pressure and cholesterol are high, but Doc's put me on medicine for the blood pressure and a diet for the cholesterol, although I don't know about the diet. You have to eat a lot of fish. I don't mind fish, but not so much." Joni heard Ceila pause to catch her breath.

"Well, that's good. How're Sarah and the kids?"

"Just fine. She sends her love. I want you to come for dinner tomorrow night."

Joni's mind raced. "I don't know. I've got some tentative plans for this weekend."

"You're just like your mother," her aunt interrupted. "When you're telling a white one, your voice goes up. Now I know you don't have any plans. I'm telling you you're having dinner with me. We need to talk."

"What about?"

"Things."

"What kinds of things?" Joni persisted.

"Just things."

"I'm not going to let you hang up," Joni insisted, "until you tell me what kinds of things."

"Things I've been hearing over here in Bayport. Two words: *Carin Chase*." Her aunt said the name slowly to emphasize it.

Joni rested her lips against the top of her hand. "Oh." Joni was unsure what to say next.

"She's saying things over here that I want to talk to you about."

"What kinds of things?"

"Joni, you're just being difficult. I don't want to talk about this stuff on the telephone. I may be seventy-eight years old, but I read all those magazines. You don't know who might be listening."

Joni laughed in spite of the gravity of the situation. "I suspect you're right. What time?"

"About five."

"You realize, Auntie, that Dr. Claymont's attorney has admonished me not to talk to anyone about this."

"Nonsense. You're not just talking to anyone, you're talking to your aunt," Ceila said before she hung up.

Joni sat staring at the telephone. She put the receiver back when it started buzzing at her. She toyed with the idea of calling Jackie, but resisted. "No," she said to the telephone. "I'm calling her for all the wrong reasons."

Saturday morning, Joni got up early. She had felt anxious all night, uncertain what her aunt wanted to talk about. She knew it wasn't about her being gay; her aunt had known that for most of Joni's adult life. In fact, her aunt had told her she'd figured it out before Joni had. She smirked at herself in the mirror as she got ready to go to her aunt's house. Her aunt had always prided herself on being a thoroughly modern woman. When Joni told her she was gay, her aunt had simply said, "I knew that. I watch *Oprah*." She wondered what kind of havoc Carin was creating with her mouth. Somehow she had suspected that Carin wouldn't suffer this indignity in silence.

When Joni arrived at the house, her aunt was standing outside waiting for her. "Hi, dearie." She gave Joni a smothering hug.

Joni hugged her back. "Missed you."

"You look tired."

"Stress," Joni reflected gloomily.

"I can see that. That woman's mouth has been operating like a well-oiled drill," Ceila said sourly. Joni gave her aunt a strained smile. "Come on." Ceila linked her arm through Joni's, and they walked quietly into the kitchen. "Supper's ready."

"It smells wonderful in here. What can I do?"

"Sit." Ceila pointed at the already-set table.

"How are you feeling?"

"Everyone asks me that. I tell them fine."

"Everyone asks you that because everyone is concerned about you."

"I'm fine. I go see Doc every couple of weeks now. He checks my heart, blood pressure. Grunts and says I'm fine."

"Good. At least you're going to see him."

"I don't really have much choice. That daughter of mine all but hijacks me and makes me go."

"She's probably afraid they'll put you back in the hospital. I heard you were a lousy patient. Didn't like the food, the television, the fact that the nurses woke you up at night to check your signs."

"I hated it." Ceila sniffed. "Doctor said for me to get some rest. Next thing I know they're shoving a thermometer in my mouth. Fall back to sleep, they're waking me up to take my blood pressure. I told that young thing it was up 'cause she kept waking me up."

Joni laughed. "I'm just glad it wasn't as serious as it could have been."

"Me too," Ceila said more seriously as she set the food on the table. "Now eat," she said as she handed Joni the various dishes.

"Oh," Joni enthused after she took a bite. "These green beans are wonderful. I expect they're from your garden."

"Yes, they are," Ceila beamed. "The last of the summer crop."

"So what did you want to talk about?"

"Let's eat first. I don't want you to get indigestion," Ceila said, passing the dish to Joni. They chatted about her aunt's garden and about her daughter, Sarah. Joni talked about the clinic, but avoided talking about Carin.

"Some more scallops?" her aunt asked, handing her the dish.

"No thanks, I couldn't eat another bite. This was wonderful, Auntie. Thanks."

"Good." Ceila got up and started to clear the table.

"I'll help," Joni said.

"I don't need you to help. Just sit there and keep me company."

Joni and Ceila sat down on the large swing that hung in her aunt's yard. Ropes as thick as her wrists were attached to a huge maple tree. They sat quietly swinging back and forth.

"This is so peaceful," Joni said wistfully.

Ceila reached for Joni's hand and entwined her fingers in hers. "I never, ever, in my darkest moments thought something like this would happen," Joni said to her aunt. "You know it isn't true."

"I know."

Joni sighed.

"She's not from around here, so she doesn't have a clue that if she tells one person the news will get back eventually. She told Carmen at the beauty salon. Well, you know Carmen and I have been friends for years. So Carmen told me."

"What has she been saying?"

Joni listened as her aunt recounted Carin's charge that Joni and Jackie were lovers and that was why Carin had been forced out of a promotion. She also claimed that Jackie had tried to make a pass at her several times, something she had rejected. "So I called her up," Ceila said as she finished her story.

"You did what?" Joni stopped the swing with her feet and turned to her aunt.

"You heard me, I called her up. Told her that she wasn't from around here and that she'd better stop spreading lies about you. I told her if she had any proof she'd better march right over and show me, or I'd wash her mouth out with soap."

Joni's shock turned to laughter. "What'd she say?"

"Kept saying it was true. I kept telling her she was a liar. She hung up on me," Ceila sputtered. "I was about to call her back. You know what? She never came over with her proof."

"That's because it never happened." Joni looked earnestly at her aunt. "But she's going to do a lot of damage with this, and you know it and I know it."

"I know," Ceila said compassionately. "Some people already believe it."

"I know."

"What I can't understand is why she's doing this. The Chase family has been here as long as our family. They've never been this kinda people before. I saw Darrel's mother, Ella, at the store the other day. She won't even look me in the eyes."

"'Cause she believes it?"

"I don't think so." Joni watched as her aunt tried to put into words what she was thinking. "I think she's embarrassed. But she doesn't know what to do about it. The woman is everywhere. I know the family was real unhappy when Darrel married her."

"She knows that."

"I hear it's been a real strain. Folks say Darrel is spreading the same lies she is. 'Course he only knows what she's said. But I don't think his folks believe it."

"I just wish someone here knew more about her. It's be nice if she had some clandestine secrets she was running away from."

"Everyone has secrets. Some people's secrets are more savage than others. What I can't understand is why she's doing it."

"Jealousy, flaming anger, resentment. Some twisted need to have everyone attracted to her. All she ever talked about when we had lunch together was Darrel. It was Darrel this, Darrel that. It was after she'd seen Dana." Joni paused. "I don't know if you know her. She's a Bradley. She and Jackie lived together."

"My land, yes. Beautiful girl. 'Course haven't seen her as an adult, but I expect she's just as pretty."

"She is beautiful, sophisticated, worldly. Anyway, Carin seemed to have this perverted rivalry going on with this woman. Every time Dana stopped by the office to either pick Jackie . . .Dr. Claymont up or just to see her aunt, Carin was fixated on the woman. Compared their figures, their faces. It was strange. She'd go on about it the entire lunch hour. I got to the point where I took a book, but it didn't stop her. She'd talk right through my reading." Joni stopped short of telling about her own mental comparison with both Dana and Carin. How she'd been the round pea between the two angular pods.

"I've been thinking about this, every since I saw Darrel's mother. That's why I wanted to talk to you."

"What's that?" Joni looked questioningly at her aunt.

"Talking to Ella. We're not friends, but we've known each other forever. I've been to her house. We both belong to Friends of the Library, and we're both in Star. But I wanted to ask you first."

Joni scratched her eyebrow. "I don't know. I can't see that it would hurt, but maybe I'd better have Jack . . .Dr. Claymont run it past her attorney first. This is beyond me," Joni reflected gloomily.

Ceila patted her hand. "Why don't you ask her?"

Joni said nothing as they swung back and forth. She watched as the last of that day's sun began to drop below the horizon. The cumulus clouds inched slowly across the sky. When she was younger she used to lie on her back and try to find images and figures in the clouds. "I love looking at the clouds. In Boston, I never had time to look up at the clouds. Most of the time I was too busy looking at where I was going."

Ceila followed her gaze. "I couldn't imagine living anywhere else, but here." Her aunt paused and then took a deep breath. "You know what I'm most worried about?"

"What?"

"You."

"Me?" Joni gasped. "Don't worry about me, Auntie, worry about Jack . . .Dr. Claymont."

"That's what I'm worried about, sweetie. You and the doctor. That's the third time you've refused to say her first name."

Joni turned toward her aunt. "Auntie, there's nothing going on. I'd never lie to you about something like that. I got the promotion because Vera, that's Dr. Claymont's office manager, suggested that I be put in charge. I haven't slept with her. I wouldn't do that," Joni's eyes filled with tears.

"I know. I'm not talking about what that nasty woman has been saying about you. What I'm talking about is you, child. I saw the look in your eyes when she came into my hospital room that night. It was the same look you got in your eyes when Alex came into the room. You've fallen in love, and that's what I'm worried about."

Joni turned back and looked out across her aunt's garden. The picked cornstalks that had been green and growing all summer were brown and withering in the September sun. "Is it that obvious?"

"To me. But then I've known you your whole life."

Joni closed her eyes, her mind folding into the rhythm of the swing and the squeak of the rope as they swung back and forth, back and forth. "You needn't worry, Auntie. Nothing can come of this." Joni brushed a tear from her cheek.

"Come here." Ceila held out her arms, and Joni laid her face against her aunt's shoulder and cried.

"This is so stupid," she said, her words muffled.

Ceila patted her hair. "Falling in love is never stupid. It just hurts a lot some times."

Joni sat up and wiped her face on the back of her sleeve. "In this instance it's stupid. She doesn't have a clue how I feel."

"Why don't you tell her."

"I can't," Joni gasped. "Not now. With everything she's going through, she doesn't need to know that I've fallen hopelessly in love with her. In fact, she'd probably run." Joni felt a pang of regret. "Remember, that's what started all of this. I'm supposed to have slept with her." Joni thought about the sleepless nights she had had since this had happened. She'd wondered what would have happened if Carin hadn't unleashed this monster of a lie. She knew that Jackie was still getting over Dana and was, in some ways, still in love with

Marianne. Marianne had been her soul mate. Joni sighed, the weight of her thoughts ponderously heavy on her. "There're just too many women in her life."

"I don't understand."

Joni told her about Dana and her three-year commitment to living in Greece. She also told her aunt about Jackie's long relationship with Marianne.

"What are you going to do?" her aunt asked when she finished.

"I don't know. Right now, I'm going to help her get through this Human Rights thing." Joni told her aunt about the timetable for Jackie answering Carin's complaint and the possibility of a hearing. "After that, pray. Pray that the investigator believes Jackie and me and not Carin."

"And then?"

"I've been talking to my former supervisor in Boston, mostly to ask her if she knew anyone in Atlanta who might have worked with Carin, but also" — Joni chewed on her bottom lip — "I'm thinking about going back there for a while, going back to the hospital."

"Is that wise? I've never known you to run from something."

"I've never been in a situation where I'm in love with someone and they are plagued by all kinds of ghosts . . . Marianne, Dana. There are just too many complications in her life." Joni shivered.

"Let's go inside. It's getting cold out here." Ceila rubbed her bare arms.

Joni brushed her sleeve against her face to wipe away the last of the tears.

"Thank you, Auntie. It's times like this I miss my mother the most."

"I know, dearie. It's times like this I miss her too. She was a wonderful sister. You're so much like her. That doctor would be lucky to have someone like you in her life."

Joni smiled cynically. "I think she's had enough of any kind of woman in her life."

Ceila held the screen door open for them. "Go splash some cold water on your face. You'll feel better. I'll get us something to drink."

They sat quietly in the kitchen sipping a cup of tea. "Thanks, Auntie."

"For making you cry? I'm sorry —"

"No." Joni looked at her aunt. "For making me say out loud what I'd been thinking about for weeks. Now, at least I can start making some decisions."

"Don't make any decisions now. Wait. Wait until all this stress is behind you," her aunt urged.

"Sometimes, I wonder if that will ever happen." She finished her tea and rubbed her forehead. "I think I'll go home. Suddenly I'm really, really tired." She kissed her aunt on the cheek.

On the drive home, Joni replayed her conversation with her aunt over and over in her mind. Somewhere in the past few weeks, she had fallen in love with Jackie. "Or maybe," she said out loud to the trees that raced past her car window, "maybe I've been in love with her from the beginning."

She pulled into her driveway and let herself in the house. She was disappointed when she saw that her answering machine did not have any messages. She thought about Jackie and wondered what she was doing. She put the thought out of her mind. She looked at the clock and chuckled. It was nine o'clock on a Saturday night, and all she wanted to do was go to bed and sleep the sleep of the innocent.

Chapter 17

Jackie was satisfied with the rhythm they'd established at the office. She and Sondra were alternating weekends on call, and for the first time in months she'd felt relieved that some of the medical pressure was gone. Although she felt good about that, she still was waiting anxiously for the next letter from the Human Rights Commission. Her attorney had filed their responses to Carin's allegations; now it was up to the investigator to respond.

"Hey, Lady Doctor." Sondra poked her head in Jackie's office. "You look tired, worn, and despairing."

"Thanks." But Jackie knew that her friend was teasing. "I

feel all of the above and more. Come in. How about a cup of tea?"

"No, thanks," Sondra dropped in one of the chairs and draped her long leg over the arm. "Still nothing?" Jackie looked at her friend. Sondra was more than six feet tall, but angular and leggy, not overgrown with weight. Unlike Dana's exotic red hair, Sondra's was a meld of red, blond, and brown. But there was no mistaking the freckles; there were few white patches on her nose, cheeks, or arms.

"My attorney filed the response just a few days ago. This is the first of November, and she seems to think we'll hear something by the end of the month."

"This is so inexplicably mysterious to me. I realize that this all came out of the sixties feminist movement, the same movement that made it a lot easier for people like you and me to attend medical school, but I never expected it would affect us so intimately," Sondra mused.

"Me either. I've read about sexual harassment cases over the years. Some of the more egregious cases found their way into newspapers. But talk about numb, I was the numbest. I never realized it was something that could be used against me," Jackie said warily. "In a small clinic, you get to know the employees probably a lot better than in a large clinic or hospital. We all suffer when their kids are sick or when something tragic happens. Now if a nurse comes to me crying because something cataclysmic is happening in her life, I'm going to resist touching her, even if it's just to give her a comfort hug. What are we supposed to do, Sondra? Hire only male nurses?"

"I don't know. Then do you hire only gay male nurses? I honestly don't know. At Harvard, we have a written policy that makes it clear what professors can and cannot do. But at a small clinic like this, I'm sure you don't even have a written personnel policy."

"We don't, but we will. That is something I've asked my

169

Portland attorney to draw up." Jackie rubbed her palms against her eyes.

"Jacks, I know you won't listen to me, but why don't you take a few days off? Go somewhere."

"I can't, Sondra. Work is diversion therapy; it's the only thing keeping me sane right now. Otherwise I'd like to sit in the middle of a road somewhere and scream."

"I wouldn't advise that here, but somewhere up in the woods you might get away with it." Jackie noted that her friend's eyes glistened with humor. "Although pity the bears and moose."

Jackie laughed. "You could be right. I was thinking..." Jackie paused to organize her thoughts. "Depending on how this comes out, I might take a week and go away."

"Away, as in to Greece?"

"No," Jackie said cautiously. "That part of my life is over. This is going to sound bizarre, but my friend Kristan said it best. She said that Dana had to happen when she did, but it was never meant to be forever." Jackie held out her hand. "Dana is like trying to hold water in your hand. When you spread out your fingers, it spills away. She came into my life and filled it with passion and hope, but it was never meant to be forever."

"I feel as though I should have some sage maxim to offer here, but the most I can come up with is, are you sure?"

"Yes, I'm sure." Jackie smiled to cover her sadness. "I'm not happy, but I'm sure."

"I like Joni."

"Yes, she's been steadfast though all of this."

"I was thinking..." Sondra and Jackie looked up when they heard the courteous knock on the door.

"Come in," Jackie said.

Jackie noticed Vera's pallid look and felt her heart fading. "Your attorney is on line one."

"Stay, Vera. We might as well all hear this," Jackie said as she pushed the button on her speaker.

"Pat? Just to let you know that Vera is here with me and Dr. Sondra Stern. What's the word?" Jackie felt as though someone had a choke hold on her windpipe. She licked her dry lips.

"We're going to hearing. I spoke with the investigator just a few minutes ago. He said you both have convincing statements, so he thinks the only way to resolve it is to hear testimony in person."

"When?"

"Next week. I asked him not to delay it. I suspect you'd rather get this over with."

"Yes, I would."

"I'll be in touch. I need to talk with you, Joni, and Vera prior to the hearing. We'll go over her allegations and your statements. Anyway, I wish the news had been better. But, Jackie, we're going to win this."

"Thanks, Pat." Jackie pushed the button on her telephone.

"I'll tell Joni," Vera said.

"Thanks." Jackie waited until Vera closed the door, then put her head in her hands and began to sob.

Sondra walked around the desk and folded her friend into her arms. "I'm so sorry." She let Jackie cry.

Jackie stepped back and grabbed some Kleenex. "I haven't cried like this since Marianne died." She began crying again, ever more distressed.

"I know," Sondra said gently. "It's been like an overheated steam boiler around here, and you've not been under this much pressure since she died. This would crush anyone's spirit."

"Everything I am is on the line. My reputation, my credibility." Jackie hiccuped. "Everything I've worked for could be wrecked. There is some kind of destructive edge to all this because even if I win and the investigator believes me, I lose. What kind of person would play that kind of maniacal game with another person's existence?"

"I don't know." Sondra felt frustrated at her inability to help her friend.

"What's even more scary," Jackie said as she wiped her eyes, "I've put out feelers with medical people I know and so has Joni to see if this woman has some kind of past, and there's been nothing. I even called the hospital where she was last employed, talked to the personnel director there. Nothing. Even Jennifer called a friend of hers who's an assistant district attorney somewhere in Georgia, and nothing. Joni's aunt tried to talk with Darrel's mother, but there's nothing."

"No one can be this mean and not have some kind of past. She —" Sondra stopped when she heard the knock.

"Come in." Jackie threw the balled up Kleenex in her wastebasket.

"I'm sorry. I thought you were alone." Joni started to close the door.

"Wait." Sondra said. "She is. You two need to talk, and" — she glanced sideways at her watch — "I have rounds to make. Call me tonight," she told Jackie.

Joni took in Jackie's blotchy red face. "Vera told me."

Jackie looked at her wearily. "This is going to get messier before it gets better."

"I know. I feel so helpless. Is there anything I can do?" Jackie read the compassion in Joni's eyes.

"Just be there. Help me convince the investigator that this is a monstrous lie by a pathetic human being."

"God, I wish . . ." Joni could feel her emotions crumbling. "Look," she started again, but a sob escaped before she could bite it back. "I'm so sorry," she sobbed. "I don't mean to cry like this."

Jackie walked around the desk and held her arms open. Joni put her head against Jackie's shoulder and cried. Jackie had a vision of her conversation moments before with Sondra about comforting an employee, but how, she thought, could she disregard that side of her personality. "That's okay," Jackie said gently. "I think there's room for both of us to cry today." She held Joni against her. She could feel her warmth, Joni's face hot against her neck. Joni looked up at her, tears streaming down her face, and Jackie felt a barrier fracture inside. She pulled Joni's mouth to hers and kissed her passionately, her tongue seeking and then finding Joni's. She crushed her hard against her. Joni gasped, and Jackie stepped back, bumping up against her filing cabinet. "I'm sorry," she said. "I can't believe I did that." Jackie looked around her as if she'd awakened in an unfamiliar environment.

"It was my fault." Joni faltered. Jackie noticed her eyes as wide as a kitten and just as unguarded. "God, I've ruined everything. I'm so sorry," Joni said as she backed out of Jackie's office.

Jackie just stared at the open door, too anesthetized to move, her thoughts careening around her brain. "What the hell happened?" she whispered. She walked to her door and quietly closed it. "What the hell happened?"

Chapter 18

Jackie and Vera arrived early at the state building where the hearing was to be held. On the three-hour trip to Augusta, Vera had related her concerns about Joni. Jackie had not commented. Ever since the kiss in the office, Joni seemed to have created a mental cloister that made her unreachable. Jackie had tried to talk to her, but Joni recoiled from any situation where the two were alone. Jackie and Vera were sitting on a long wooden bench outside the hearing room when her attorney arrived.

"Did you have a good drive down?" the attorney inquired.

"Yes, fine," Jackie answered distractedly.

"Is Joni here?"

"She's driving down herself," Vera answered. "She said she had errands to run."

Pat looked questioningly at Jackie. "She's coming?"

"She said she'd be here. I trust that," Jackie said solemnly.

"Why, hi." Jackie heard the friendly voice before she saw Carin. "Why, hi, Vera. You here too? Isn't this just too silly. I make a little bitty complaint, and they drag us all the way down here. Why, I told Darrel to stay home," Carin chattered.

"Carin Chase," Pat held her hand out to the woman. "My name is Pat Harrington. I am representing Dr. Claymont in this, and I really don't think it's appropriate for you to be speaking to my client right now."

"That's right. You're acting like this is some kind of baked-bean supper," Vera spat out. "Why I'd —"

"That's enough," Pat held up her hand to silence Vera. "There's a conference room over there. Why don't you two" — she nodded to Jackie and Vera — "wait in there while I check on the investigator."

"Well, where should I wait?" Jackie could hear the whiny hurt in Carin's voice and wondered at how often she had heard it at the clinic when Carin had not gotten her way.

"In hell," Jackie heard Vera mutter under her breath as they walked into the conference room. Pat closed the door after them.

Jackie watched Carin through the glass door. She patted her hair and adjusted her black skirt over her hips. She had on a black blouse and matching black jacket. Even her nylons were a shiny black. She reminded Jackie of a panther, one of the few cats to strike from above. Carin suddenly looked up and met Jackie's eyes, and Jackie saw a feral rage before the mask was pulled back in place. She saw Carin smile and then walk up the hallway. Jackie got up and opened the door just as Carin was reaching out to hug Joni. "We're in here," Jackie said to her nurse.

"Why, honey, don't you look a sight. You've lost weight.

Your eyes are all red. My, my," Carin said as she watched Joni walk toward the conference room. "My, my," she said with a smile on her face.

"You okay?" Jackie asked Joni.

"Just a cold. I didn't expect to see her so soon."

"Friendly little thing," Vera spat out. "She reminds me of a story a Passamaquoddy told me." Vera launched into the story without encouragement. "This young Native American went into the mountains as part of his rite of passage to be a man, and the temperature dropped. He unrolled his sleeping bag, and this rattlesnake slithered out from under a rock. The rattler asked to sleep with the boy, and the boy said no, fearing the snake would bite him. The snake pleaded he was cold and promised he wouldn't hurt the boy. They slept together all night, and in the morning when the sun came out, the snake slithered out from the blanket and thanked the boy and then bit him. When the boy cried out about the promise the snake had made, the rattler said, but I'm a snake. That woman's a snake."

Jackie chuckled in spite of the gravity of the situation. "I'm not sure if that story made me feel better or worse." She looked at Joni. "How are you?"

"Fine, really." Joni's smile was strained. "I've just had a small cold. I thought, if you didn't mind, I'd like to take tomorrow off."

"Of course —" Jackie stopped when she saw Pat at the door.

"We're ready," Pat said as she opened the door.

The three women followed Pat into the examiner's room. Carin was already seated alone at a table. Pat directed Jackie, Vera, and Joni to sit at the other table.

"Good morning." The examiner cleared his throat. "My name is Brad Pollock, and I am an investigator for the Maine Human Rights Commission. The format today is simple. I will read the charges Mrs. Chase has made, then I will question her. After that, I will question" — he looked down at his papers — "Dr. Jackie Claymont. After that any witnesses she or Mrs. Chase have brought also will be questioned. This is an informal setting; we don't sequester witnesses. Once I have listened to all the testimony, then it takes a week or two and I will render my decision in writing, a copy of which will be available to anyone in this room. If I should rule against Dr. Claymont, then there are certain legal avenues that Mrs. Chase may pursue, including suing to get not only her job back, but also any back pay she lost. She can also ask for additional compensation. Does everyone understand?"

Jackie noticed that Carin was smiling. "Ask away, sugar," she said to the investigator. "I have nothing to hide."

They all listened attentively as the investigator read the charges against Jackie, the same charges that had been included in the letters she had received from the Maine Human Rights Commission.

"You were hired, let's see," the investigator said as he again looked at his papers. "In February, February sixth to be exact. Why don't you start with that day?"

"Yes. Well, it actually started a few days before that," Carin corrected the investigator. "I went into the office and dropped off my résumé. Jackie . . .Dr. Claymont called me a few days later and invited me in for an interview. We hit it off just fine, and she hired me a few days later. Everything was fine until Vera, that's her office manager, came back. She'd been on some kind of a cruise with her mother. Anyway, shortly after that, about a week or so, they hired Joni, and that's when everything started to get weird."

"What do you mean 'weird'?" the investigator inquired.

"She'd be hanging out in the doctor's office, things like that. Then, in April, April fifth. I remember it so well." Jackie watched as Carin looked at a paper she had pulled from her handbag and then closed her eyes and physically gave a shudder. "It was in the morning, and Jackie, Dr. Claymont, and I were in the examining room, and that's when she tried to grab me."

"What do you mean by 'grab'?"

"She was standing behind me, and she ran her hands over my back, and then she started to kiss my hair and the back of my neck. When I tried to pull away, she turned me around and tried to kiss me. Kept saying things like how beautiful I was, am." Carin patted her hair. "I pushed her away. I was just so shocked by what she did."

"Then what happened."

"I left the examining room."

"Did you report this incident to anyone?"

"No, I was just so scared. Plus, who'd believe me? Vera's always taking Jackie's side. She has to if she wants to keep her job." Jackie noticed that Carin's eyes glimmered with malevolence.

"Did you tell your husband? I believe in your report you said you are married."

"No," she said haughtily. "I didn't tell Darrel. I was just too ashamed. Plus, he'd have made me quit after he'd popped the doctor in the nose. I couldn't quit," she said sadly. "I'm helping my husband start his plumbing and heating business."

"In the doctor's statement she said you invited her to your house for dinner in late April? If you were afraid of the doctor, why'd you do that?"

Carin sighed expressively. "I thought it would give her a chance to see how happily married I was . . . am. Then she'd leave me alone. But she kept trying to touch me. Made remarks about my body, about how sexy I am. Said I was a real turn on. I kept telling her not to say such things. 'Course I was afraid to say it too loud, what with my husband sound asleep just a few feet away from us. She put her hand on my leg, and I pushed her away. She wouldn't leave me alone, kept saying things and everything. I was scared 'cause I didn't want to make her mad. I was scared she'd fire me. So I tried to laugh it off, pretend it was a joke. But when she got ready to leave, she grabbed me, tried to kiss me. I was shocked. I didn't know what to do. I was scared, and my heart was racing. I pretended the kiss was just an accident, and then she left."

"What time was that?"

"Around nine."

"And you never told your husband?"

"I couldn't. Darrel would have killed her."

"Did you tell anyone else? A friend? Someone in your family?"

"No, I was too ashamed."

The investigator studied Carin for a moment and asked, "Then what happened?"

"Well, it happened two times at the clinic after that, once on June fourteenth and another time, the day after the Fourth of July. Each time I told the doctor I wasn't a queer. Well, I didn't use that word, but she knew what I meant." Carin talked on for a long time, about Jackie's sexuality and how much it repulsed her. "But she wouldn't leave me alone." Carin hesitated. "Then one time after that, I walked into the doctor's office. I thought everyone had left and I found her" — she pointed at Joni — "and the doctor doing some of the most awful things. Please don't make me describe it, but it was sexual." Carin stopped and sucked air into her lungs. "I ran from the clinic. It was right after that Joni was promoted to senior nurse and I was forced to take orders from her. It was terrible. I finally had to quit. And this is the hardest part." Carin put her face in her hands. "It's made it real hard on Darrel and me. Why, we almost lost the business 'cause I didn't have my paycheck. Plus, Darrel's been upset about all of this and hasn't been concentrating on his work."

"Did Dr. Claymont or Joni speak to you afterward about what you'd seen?"

"No," Carin said sharply. "I don't think they saw me. They were so wrapped up in what they were doing. It was disgusting, just disgusting."

"After that?"

"I told Darrel. He was just incensed. I thought he was going to go down to the clinic and shoot the doctor. But I persuaded him to stay calm. He's the one who called the attorney, and the attorney said to file a grievance with you." Carin smiled at the investigator for the first time. "Darrel wanted to hire the man, but it was going to cost fifteen hundred dollars up front, and we couldn't afford that. I told Darrel, well, I'd just come here and tell the truth and you'd believe me. And I'll tell you, I think this woman owes me. I haven't been able to find another job, and so I just know you'll make it right." Carin leaned forward as she spoke directly to the investigator. Jackie noted that Carin's eyes were brimming with sincerity.

The investigator sorted through several pages and pulled hers up. "In your original complaint, you didn't mention specific dates, but now you do."

"Well, I had to sit down and think about it. And when I hadn't heard from you, I spoke with the attorney again. He said it would help my case if I remembered exactly when these incidents occurred. So" — she reached into her handbag again — "I've filed an amended complaint." She handed it to him.

"Anything else?" he said after he'd read the new complaint. He handed it to Pat to read.

"Isn't that enough?"

"Thank you." The investigator turned from Carin to Jackie. "Dr. Claymont?"

"I'm not certain how to answer this," Jackie said, "because it's all fantasy."

"Can you prove that?" the investigator asked.

Jackie told the investigator that she'd never sought Carin out for anything other than in her role as a nurse at the clinic. She told about the dinner at Carin's house and how she had rushed to get out of there. "In fact, I do have proof on that one. I left her house around seven and I was at the hospital by seven-thirty. I ran into Joni there."

"Lies," Carin shouted. "She's lying."

Jackie stopped as she watched Vera say something to Pat and then leave.

"No, she's not," Joni spoke for the first time. "You can check the hospital records. My aunt was admitted suffering with chest pains."

"Can anyone else confirm this?" the investigator asked.

"My aunt," Joni said. "Dr. Larson was there. That's my aunt's doctor. In fact," she looked at Jackie, "the two of you talked."

Vera slipped quietly back into the room and handed a book to Pat. Pat looked at several of the pages Vera was showing her.

"Excuse me," Pat interrupted Joni. "I'd like the doctor's office manager to address some of the specifics of this new complaint Mrs. Chase handed you. I realize it's out of order, but as you said, this is an informal hearing," she said to the investigator.

He nodded to Vera.

"On the date in April that Carin, Mrs. Chase, mentioned" — Vera paged through the calendar — "Dr. Claymont was not in the office." Vera looked at the investigator. "She was in Bangor at a Maine Medical Conference sponsored by the hospital. On the June date Carin mentioned" — Vera turned the pages again — "Dr. Claymont was at the office all day. But on the fifth of July, Jackie wasn't in at all that day. She'd had two medical emergencies and was in surgery all morning and afternoon. I know because I had to rebook all of the patients who had appointments at the clinic, and I have all kinds of notes in the margin telling where I put everyone."

"May I see that?"

"Absolutely." Vera glared at Carin as she walked up to the investigator's table and handed him the book.

"Well, I could be wrong on just a few of those dates," Carin interrupted. "Let me see." Jackie watched as Carin wiped sweat from her upper lip. She fumbled in her bag and pulled out a calendar. "Well, yes," she said sweetly. " I was off by a few days. It must have been the fifteenth of June. And the other incident might have been before the holiday." She frowned at her calendar. "Yes, that's right."

Pat rose as she spoke to the investigator. "In view of this information, I think these charges against my client should be dropped. Mrs. Chase is on a fishing trip, and right now for her to assure us it was one date and then another, well —"

"I just made a simple mistake," Carin snarled.

"I have to agree with Mrs. Harrington," the investigator said.

"Wait a minute," Carin said more fiercely. "I said I made a mistake."

"Mrs. Chase, I think you need to calm down."

"I am calm," she raged. "I'm so calm I could scream." She stared rudely at Jackie. "You're not getting away with this," she said bitterly. "That job was mine. Why, I was nice to you even though I knew you were committing a sin against God."

"The only sin here," Pat said rudely to Carin, "is the sin of lying. I ask that this hearing end and that you find in favor of my client."

"I demand," Carin shouted suddenly and aggressively, "I demand you sit here and listen to me."

"I think this is over," the investigator said.

Carin threw him a filthy look. "They're lying. I . . ." there was a long silence as Carin watched the investigator collect his papers and place them in a manila file. "I said they're lying," she growled.

"Mrs. Chase, you're wasting my time. This case is dismissed. I find in favor of the defendant, Dr. Jackie Claymont."

Carin slammed her fist down on the table and tried to speak, but all that came out of her mouth was a loud sob. "No, no," she sobbed over and over again. "She —"

Pat motioned for Jackie, Joni, and Vera to follow her. Pat closed the door on the still sobbing Carin.

"Is it over?" Jackie looked at her questioningly.

"Yes, it's time to celebrate." Pat smiled. "Let's get out of here before she makes another scene." They followed Pat out to the parking lot.

Jackie looked at Vera, "I have you to thank for this."

"Not really. Pat told me to bring your appointment book along just in case."

"Then I have you to thank," Jackie said to the attorney.

"Just doing my job. I had a feeling that dates might come up." She smiled at Jackie. "Let's just say if they did, I wanted to be ready. But it's time for you to celebrate."

"Why do I feel so unlike celebrating?" Jackie looked from Vera to Joni.

"Because you're tired," Vera said gently.

"Congratulations, Jackie," Joni said.

"I don't feel like I won a thing," Jackie said sourly. "This still will be in the paper."

"I suspect when the investigator is finished writing his report," Pat shook her head, "Carin's going to look really bad. I read these cases all the time, and an investigator does not like being lied to. That woman has a really destructive edge, and what a raging temper. Go home, Jackie. It's over."

"Come on." Vera took Jackie by the arm. "That's her van over there. I want to get out of here before she makes another scene."

Jackie shook Pat's hand. "Thank you." Jackie noticed Joni say something to Vera.

"See you later?" she asked Joni as she stood by her car.

"Yes, later. I asked Vera if I could go straight home. This cold has me in its grip."

"Get some rest," Jackie said.

"You, too," Joni said softly.

Chapter 19

Joni spent the next few days in bed with her aunt fretting over her. Ceila had called to see how the hearing had gone, and when she had heard Joni's voice, Ceila insisted Joni needed her. Ceila had also called Vera, who had told Joni to take as much time as she needed. Vera had said they'd hired a temporary nurse, over Jackie's protestations, and that things at the clinic were back to normal.

"So what are your plans?" Ceila asked, handing Joni yet another glass of orange juice.

"I can't drink any more juice," Joni complained. "I hardly got the last one down."

"Vitamin C. You need Vitamin C."

"I'm taking Vitamin C in tablet form. So I am getting enough Vitamin C," she sniffed.

"Posh, that's not the real stuff. You have to drink lots of fresh-squeezed orange juice and eat plenty of my homemade chicken soup. And don't change the subject. What are your plans."

"I gave Vera my notice over the telephone."

"And the doctor?"

"I expect she told her."

"That seems mighty chicken hearted. You should have spoken with her."

"Then I'm chicken hearted."

Her aunt sat down on the edge of the bed and took Joni's hand. "You're still feverish."

"I know."

"Why are you fighting this. You love her."

"I know. But it's not fair for me to add more encumbrances to her life right now. She's just come through a nasty hearing. The woman she loved chose a career over her, and, well, it's just not fair. And I know she's stewing about that investigator's report. Depending on how he writes it, she could really take a hit in her professional life."

"What's not fair is not telling her how you feel."

"No, Auntie. What's fair is my getting the hell out of her life. I've thought about this. If I reach out to her now, is she reaching back because she's in love with me or because she's hurting? I don't want to find out later it was because she's hurting."

Ceila patted her hand. "When your Uncle John and I met, we fell in love and married. I'm not saying that every day was a picnic. In fact, there were times in the early years when I thought I was going to leave him."

"Really?"

"Really. We had to work at it. So did your mom and dad. Put two people together in a house, and they have to learn how to live together. It doesn't just happen. Life seemed so uncomplicated then," Ceila wistfully said. "Look around you today. Marriages seem to come apart at the seams over the slightest provocation. Women put careers ahead of marriage and relationships." Ceila shrugged. "Both parents working. Kids being raised by day-care centers. I wonder how much all of this is going to change us as a society?"

"I don't know. But I wonder if it just seemed so much simpler then because there were fewer choices. Unskilled women stuck in dead-end marriages." Joni used her aunt's words to paint a different picture. "Both parents having to work just to give their children the things Daddy and Uncle John were able to provide with their single jobs."

"I guess, when you put it that way, it does make a difference. So what are your plans?"

"I plan to go to work on Monday, work the week, and then leave. I have to be in Boston the following Monday. So right now I have to get over this cold and pack. Actually, I guess I can come back here and pack everything else up later. I'll take some things with me; I plan to stay with friends until I can find an apartment. It's not as if I have to find something immediately."

"Well, you're spending Thanksgiving with Sarah and the family and me."

Joni groaned. "I'm not very good company right now."

"You don't have a choice, young lady. Now drink your orange juice."

Joni started to feel better by the weekend, and by Sunday night she actually thought she might live. Her aunt had gone home Saturday, and Joni had spent the weekend reading. She usually reveled in her reading, but not this time. Even a Dr. Scarpetta mystery didn't hold her attention. She kept thinking about leaving. "It's the right thing to do," she kept repeating like a mantra all weekend.

Monday morning, she met Vera who was just unlocking the office door. "How're you feeling?" Vera asked sympathetically.

"Better. Well enough to return to work."

"Your aunt called and said you really had a fever." Vera switched on the lights and turned up the heat in the waiting room.

Joni chuckled. "Is that all she called about?"

"We talked about a number of things, actually. We knew each other years ago, before she married John Wheaton and moved over to Bayport. We did quite a bit of reminiscing. Why do you ask, dear?"

Joni looked at her oddly. "No reason. Is Jackie coming in this morning?"

"Actually, Jackie is off this week. Sondra persuaded her to spend the week in Jackman with friends. In fact, she's there for Thanksgiving."

"Did you tell her I was leaving?"

Vera looked up from the files she had been sorting. "I didn't."

Joni felt awash in disappointment. "Why?"

"I . . ." She hesitated. "Well, let's just say, I took it upon myself to not tell her. Jackie has enough to think about."

"Vera, are you angry with me?"

"Not angry, just disappointed."

"You realize what was starting to happen between Jackie and me."

"Yes."

"You know I've fallen desperately in love with her."

"Yes."

Joni could feel her temperature rising. "And yet you're disappointed with me. Why?" Joni stopped as the door opened.

"Morning, Bertha," Vera said. "Nice and early for your

appointment. Good." Vera handed Joni the file. "The nurse will take you to the examining room."

Joni looked questioningly at Vera but took the file. Vera, she realized, had dismissed her.

The next few days went quickly. Joni worked closely with Dr. Stern, and things ran smoothly. Dr. Stern never mentioned Jackie, and Joni couldn't bring herself to ask. Those times when she and Vera ended up in the lunchroom, Joni realized Vera was not going to talk about anything personal. They talked about patients and the weather. For the first time since she had arrived at the clinic, she was very lonely.

Wednesday night, Joni handed Vera her keys. "I won't be needing these anymore. Look . . ." She started to say something, then changed her mind. "I'm going to miss you."

Vera's face softened, and she hugged her. "Never mind an old crotchety woman, Joni. I just hate change, and I know Jackie is going to be hurt."

"Why didn't you tell her?"

"I don't think she could have taken one more blow last week. She's beaten, Joni. I'm hoping her spending time with her friends will lessen some of the strain. She had to get away from this. And if I'd told her you were leaving, she'd have insisted on being here. Sondra and I made the decision not to tell her. I'll take the heat when she gets back."

"I'll miss you," Joni smiled. "And you're not an old crotchety woman. We should all have someone so loyal in our lives. It's been a pleasure knowing you, Vera. I just wish this hadn't happened."

Vera hugged her again. "Me too. Keep in touch, will ya?"

"Sure."

Chapter 20

Jackie noticed all the cars parked in the lot and frowned when she didn't see Joni's. She parked in the rear and used her key to let herself in the back door. No one could have a cold lasting that long, she thought. She frowned. Maybe Joni had gotten pneumonia and no one had told her. She had thought about calling her from Jackman, but had resisted. All week all she could think about was their last time together in the office.

Jackie stopped as she thought about the kiss. She felt weak. She had been away for a week, and all she could think about was that kiss. One kiss, she thought. How many times during that week had she chided herself for focusing on it? Finally, she had convinced herself that the kiss was nothing more than a second of intimacy between two people immersed in a pool of hysteria. Her friends told her she was in love, but she refused to believe it. But they wouldn't give up. It was too soon, she had argued. Dana had only been gone five months, and it was impossible for her to fall in love so quickly. They had suggested that the kiss had awakened within her a desire to be in love again, but Jackie had rejected it as specious reasoning then, just as she was rejecting it now. Jackie stopped outside of her office door. She had spoken with Vera several times by telephone and had asked her how Joni was feeling, but all she'd say was that Joni was still ill. She stepped into her office and set her bag down. She reached for her telephone as she shrugged out of her winter jacket. "I'm in," she said to the telephone. She was putting on her lab coat when she heard the knock.

"Come in."

Vera stepped inside and closed the door. She had several messages in her hand. "Come here." Jackie held out her arms.

Vera gave her a big hug. "You look rested."

Jackie grinned sheepishly. "Just what the doctor ordered. Is Sondra in?"

"She's with patients right now. I booked a lighter schedule for you since this is your first day back." She handed the messages to Jackie.

"Good," she said as she shuffled through the messages. "I see there's a call here from Kristan. Know what that's about?"

"She didn't say, and I didn't feel it was my place to ask." Vera had her hand on the door.

"Would you send Joni back when she's free? I don't like how things ended. I should have talked to her before I left."

Vera stepped over to one of the chairs and sat down. "Joni's gone."

Jackie looked up. "What do you mean, 'she's gone'?" Jackie sat down in her desk chair and waited.

"She resigned."

"Why didn't you tell me?" Jackie asked sharply.

"Because I knew you'd try to stop her. It gets worse," Vera said smugly. "I've also hired a new nurse. Her name's Elizabeth Klein. Nice lady."

Jackie could feel her anger rising. "Vera, you have carte blanche when it comes to this office, but not my life. You should have told me. In fact —" She stopped when she heard the rap on her door.

"Come in."

"Welcome back," Sondra said as she poked her head in. She looked from Jackie to Vera and stepped inside the office. "You told her." She directed the question to Vera.

"Just now." Vera sat twisting her hands in her lap. Sondra reached out and took one of her hands in hers.

"You're angry." She said to Jackie. "But you should be angry with me, not Vera. I told Vera not to tell you she had resigned."

"Why?"

"Because, my friend, you'd just come through a sexual harassment charge, you looked like hell, and you needed some time away. You'd never have left if you'd known."

"Why are you two mucking around in my personal life. You don't know —"

"I know you've fallen in love." Sondra shot back.

Jackie sat for a long time, staring at her two friends. "Where is she?" she quietly asked Vera.

"Boston. I don't know where."

"Who would know?"

"Her aunt."

"Would you call her for me?"

"No, you call her." Vera stood up.

Jackie grimaced. Sondra grinned. "Look, I'm sorry," Jackie said by way of apology.

"I'm not mad at you for what you said earlier," Vera interrupted. "I am mucking around in your life. But someone has to because you're doing a royal fine job of screwing it up. Now if you want to find her, call Ceila."

Sondra stood up and joined Vera at the door. "I wouldn't argue with her; you'll lose." They both chuckled as they walked out the door.

Jackie shook her head and picked up the telephone book. She looked up Ceila Wheaton's name and frowned when the telephone kept ringing. She rubbed the receiver against her chin and hung up. She saw Kristan's message and dialed her office number.

"News Office," Kristan answered.

"Hey, pal."

"Jacks," Kristan almost shouted. "You're back. When'd you get in? Where are you?"

"Whoa, pal. Slow it down," Jackie laughed. It felt like the past. "I just got back today, and I'm at the office. How are things with you and Jennifer?"

There was a long silence, and then Kristan said, "We've taken a time-out. She's moved. We're still seeing the counselor you suggested, but things are not going well, actually."

"I'm sorry," Jackie said sympathetically. "Is there anything I can do?"

"No, really. At least we're still seeing each other. Look," Kristan said, "if we talk about this much longer I'm going to start bawling, and that's not why I called. I have a copy of the investigator's report. I asked the reporter in Bangor to fax it to me. I told her I would share it with you ahead of time. It'll be in tomorrow's paper."

"Aren't you violating some journalistic ethics by calling me?"

"Absolutely not. You've got to read this. The investigator did a number on Carin Chase. Stopped short of calling her a liar, but he really wrote a very unflattering piece. Suggested that her motives were something other than whistle blowing. It was really harsh. One of the worst I've ever read against a complainant."

Jackie put her head in her hands as she listened. "Will people still believe that something happened between us?"

"Only a cretin would. I mean it, Jackie, this is scathing." Jackie could hear the mild enthusiasm in her friend's voice. "What's your fax number? I'll send it over."

Jackie gave it to her and then hung up. She walked down the hall and motioned to Sondra. "The investigator's report is here. It's being faxed to me right now."

"Bad?"

"Not for us," Jackie said quietly.

Vera looked up when Jackie and Sondra joined her behind the counter. "Can I help you doctors?" she asked. She looked at the ringing fax. "Is this what I think it is?"

Jackie felt as though her skin was tingling as she waited for the machine to answer and then the pause as the two machines reached out and shook hands. She started reading as soon as the first page appeared. She pulled it off the machine and handed it to Sondra, Vera was looking over Sondra's arm.

"Wow," Sondra said.

Jackie looked over at Vera as she handed Sondra the second page; Vera's eyes were sparkling with tears. She smiled at her friend.

"Wow," Sondra exclaimed again more quietly as two of the patients curiously looked over at them. "Can we talk about this in your office?" she whispered.

"Sure," Jackie handed her the last page.

Sondra followed her back to her office. "Have Elizabeth put the patients in the examining room," Sondra said to Vera. "Then join us." She added more quietly.

Jackie reached her hands up over her head. "Thank you, God, wherever you are."

Sondra hugged her. "I've never read anything like this before. He's called her everything but a liar." Jackie looked down at the last page. "Even suggests that you might sue her."

Jackie looked as Vera entered. She reached for a Kleenex and handed it to her.

"I'm not crying," she groused.

"I didn't say you were."

"This going in tomorrow's paper?"

"Kristan says yes."

"Good. It'll put an end to the rumors once and for all. Carin's been spreading more lies, that's what Ceila told me when we last talked."

"What kinds of lies?"

"Claims you paid off the investigator. That he was biased against her. I think once this is printed it'll put those lies to rest."

Jackie frowned. "I'm not so sure."

"I do. According to Ceila, Darrel's family is waiting, but I've already heard they're calling her a liar. Ella loves her son, but she doesn't care much for his wife. I bet this is the first time someone's caught her in a lie."

Sondra patted Jackie on the back. "It's over, my friend. I've got patients waiting."

Vera picked up the ringing telephone. "Blueberry Clinic." She handed the telephone to Jackie.

"Hello," Jackie said cautiously. "Pat, have you read it?" Jackie listened. "A reporter friend of mine faxed it over. I'd say. Well, I don't know about a whitewash, but it helps." Jackie paused again as she listened. "Pat, thanks for all of your help. I don't think I could have gotten through this without you."

"You okay?" she asked Vera as she hung up.

"Absolutely. You make that other call?"

Jackie scratched the top of her head. "No answer. Look, I've got to see patients. Everything has been dumped on Sondra, and it's not fair."

"She's not complaining," Vera said at the door.

"I know, but I've got to get back to what it is I do well, doctoring." Jackie paused and smiled at Vera. "Thank you. Thank you for mucking around in every part of my life. I certainly haven't done a very good job of managing it lately."

Vera smiled as she closed the door quietly behind her.

Jackie had told Sondra to leave early, and it had been a long day. She felt invigorated for the first time in months and was looking forward to each new patient. She put the last chart on the pile next to Vera.

"Here," Vera handed her a piece of paper.

"What's this?"

"It's Joni's address, and I booked you on the last flight out of Bangor tonight. You have four hours to get to the airport, so you'd better hotfoot it."

Jackie looked from the paper to Vera.

"Yes, I'm mucking around in your life again, but like I said, someone needs to."

"What about tomorrow? I have patients to see."

"I've got most of them rescheduled. Sondra agreed. She said I should kick your butt out of here."

"Shouldn't I call her?"

"No," Vera said emphatically.

"But what if she's not there?"

"She's there."

"You've been busy."

Vera looked impatiently at the clock. "Jackie, I've known you most of your life. Now just go, don't think, don't reason, just go," Vera ordered.

"Okay, okay. I need a shower."

"You have time."

"Oh my god, what about Bob?"

"I've already made arrangements to pick her up at day care."

"You hate dogs! You'd do that for me?"

"Go." Vera pushed her. "Before I change my mind." Jackie noticed the slightest glimmer of a smile on her friend's mouth. She hugged Vera.

She ran back to her office and picked up her medical bag. Vera followed her. "What if she doesn't want me?" she said out loud. "Doesn't love me?"

"You're just going to have to convince her," Vera said confidently. Jackie smiled and gave Vera a shy kiss on the cheek. For the first time in weeks she felt young and invigorated. She had a newfound sense of freedom, and she was determined to share it with the woman she loved.

Chapter 21

Brian Adam's "I'll Always Be Right There" kept playing over and over again in Jackie's head as she waited for the ticket agent to process her ticket. That's what she wanted with Joni, a lifetime commitment.

"Here you are, Dr. Claymont," the agent said as she handed the ticket to Jackie. "The Boston flight has just landed, and they'll be boarding in about twenty minutes at gate three."

Jackie picked up her overnight bag and ticket. "Thank you." Just a couple of hours more and she would be pleading her case to Joni. She started toward the gate, ignoring the weary travelers who were rushing to the carousel to reclaim their luggage.

"Hi, what —"

Jackie stopped. "Are you doing here?" Jackie finished her sentence.

"I had to come. I had to talk to you." Jackie saw the tears in Joni's eyes. "Are you leaving for a medical convention?" She could hear the fear in Joni's voice.

"No, I was coming to find you." Jackie felt disoriented by her surroundings. She wanted to crush Joni in her arms. Kiss away the tears on her face. She looked around. People were glancing their way as they made their dash through the terminal. "Come on." Jackie took Joni by the elbow. Joni didn't say a word as they maneuvered their way across the terminal. "We need to talk privately."

Jackie walked them out the door and across the airport road to the Marriott Hotel. She handed the desk clerk her credit card and waited for him to process it.

"Here is your keycard and your room number," the desk clerk said as he circled the number on the little white envelope. " Thank you, Dr. Claymont, for staying with us."

Jackie picked up her overnight bag. "Come on," she said quietly to Joni.

Inside the room, Jackie put her bag down. Joni was standing just inside the door. "I don't want to talk. I just want to do this." Jackie gently raised Joni's chin with the edge of her finger and kissed her. "I've been thinking about this since the first time we kissed," she said against Joni's lips.

"Me too." Joni put her arms around Jackie's neck and pulled her close. Jackie felt her breath catch in her chest at the intensity of Joni's kiss. The touch of Joni's moist lips seemed exciting and new but at the same time strangely familiar. As she held Joni close, she thought about the many years they had traveled through life on parallel paths. The same hometown, similar professions, and the same lifestyle, all without ever knowing each other until the last few months. Now Joni was in her arms, and the excitement Jackie felt was enhanced by her realization that while some lovers were only for a moment, this woman was for a lifetime.

As she held her, Jackie felt many of the same feelings she had felt so many years ago in Marianne's arms. She felt excited and calm and secure at the same time. Joni's body fit closely against her own, and it communicated the urgency and excitement she had always felt when she and Marianne had come together.

"I want you so much. I love you so much. But I'm scared," Joni said, her forehead resting against Jackie's shoulder. "I don't know how you feel. I didn't think I would ever feel like this again." Jackie could hear the hesitancy in Joni's voice.

"Somewhere in this crazy mess, I fell in love with you," Jackie said gently. "All I know is" — she looked deep into Joni's radiant eyes — "I haven't thought much beyond this very minute. I love you, I want to make love to you, and I want to spend the rest of my life loving you. I feel —" Jackie stopped. She could feel a blush on her cheek. "I feel like a twenty-year-old. I don't want to be artful; I just want to devour you."

"Oh god, yes," Joni said, her lips open.

Jackie reached out and turned off the light, then gently led Joni to the bed.

They lay down fully clothed, and Jackie gently began to unbutton Joni's blouse. They both knew they would sleep little that night. And they also knew there was no need to hurry. They would caress and enjoy each other for the first time tonight. But more importantly, they would love each other always.

Jackie felt at peace for the first time in months. The woman she loved was with her, and she felt a new sense of promise about life. They had slept late and then made love again. Jackie had felt overwhelmed by Joni's hunger and her passion to please her. Now they were traveling back to Bailey's Cove. They hadn't even talked about where home would be; those life decisions would come easily for them. She felt so at one with this woman.

She reached over and touched Joni's hand. Joni's fingers curled comfortably in her hand. "Can we stop at the clinic a minute? I think Vera is probably busting a gut wondering where I am. I usually check in by now."

Joni smiled. "Of course."

Jackie turned into the clinic parking lot and stopped when she saw the van. She looked at Joni, who also had seen the vehicle.

"There are a lot of green vans in the world." Jackie could hear the cautionary tone in Joni's voice. "It doesn't mean it's her."

"Stay here."

"No," Joni opened her door. "If it's her, I want to be with you."

"It could make it worse."

"What more can she do to us?"

"Come on." Jackie said confidently.

Jackie opened the door to the clinic and saw Vera's face first. There was a tightness around her mouth. Vera nodded toward the chair. Carin was sitting there alone, reading a magazine.

"Well, well, well." Carin dropped the magazine on the floor. "The lovers return."

Jackie closed the door behind Joni. "Carin, what are you doing here."

"That's what Vera's been asking. But I wouldn't tell her. None of her business. That's what I told her." Carin walked within inches of Jackie and stared directly into her eyes. "Got some color in your cheeks. I wonder who's been doing that?" She looked over at Joni. Joni stared back at her.

"She's been here since this morning," Vera said.

"Carin, I want you out of here." Jackie stood between Carin and Joni.

"No you don't, 'cause I ain't done with you. You smeared my name all over the newspaper, and I'm going to sue you."

"I haven't even seen the newspaper this morning."

Carin waved the newspaper in Jackie's face. Jackie grabbed it out of her hand. She didn't have to read beyond the headline, it said all: INVESTIGATOR CLAIMS NURSE LIED WHEN SHE ACCUSED DOCTOR OF SEXUAL HARASSMENT.

"They lied." Carin stamped her foot. "The newspaper lied. And you did this," she hissed.

"Carin, I want you out of this office."

"What's it like, Jackie," Carin said as if she hadn't heard her. "Making love to that sack of shit when you could have had something like me?" She ran her hand over her hair.

Joni saw Jackie react and reached out a hand to her. "Don't," Joni said quietly. "She's just trying to get you to do something that will only make more problems for you. She's not worth it."

"Well, I'm worth a lot more than you, sugar," Carin snapped at her. "I'm beautiful and passionate and —"

"Then go home," Joni interrupted. "Go home to your husband and be beautiful and passionate for Darrel and leave us alone. Carin, you can't do or say anything more to hurt us. Now get the hell out of here."

"Oh no, you don't." Joni watched as Carin's smile turned to fury, and she could hear the rancor in her voice. "You are going to pay for this. I am going to make your life hell. My marriage is gone —" Carin stopped. "Well, not gone. Darrel's just upset over this article. He stormed out this morning. Said everything he'd worked for went down the toilet." Her laugh sounded hollow. "Get it? A plumber, and his work went down the toilet." She stomped around the office. "That jerk. Lately his lovemaking was as mechanical as cleaning a toilet. I just wanted to make him jealous. Now this." She waved the newspaper again. "This is your fault," she seethed. "You got this in the newspaper. Made me look like a cheap —"

"That's enough. I want you out of here." Jackie opened the door. "I want you out of here, or by God I am going to call the police."

Carin stopped. "You wouldn't do that. Just be more bad publicity."

"For you, Carin. Now leave," Jackie willed herself to keep the anger she was feeling from her voice. "Carin, just leave."

Carin dropped the newspaper on the floor. She smoothed her dress over her hips. "All I wanted to do was make Darrel a little jealous. That's all. Get him interested in me like before. He's been so worried about building his business, he forgot all about me. All he did was work and watch baseball. Too tired to do anything else. All I wanted to do was just make him jealous," she whined. She looked from Joni to Jackie. Joni could see the tears in her eyes. Then they were gone, and the anger was back. "You're disgusting, ya know that? Violate God's Word. You're sinners. Nothing but sinners."

"Well, Carin, we've got something you'll never have." Jackie walked up to her and stood very close.

"You ain't got nothing." Carin flew through the door. "You ain't got nothing," she yelled behind her.

The three of them stood silently in the waiting room until they heard Carin's tires as she screeched out of the driveway.

"Are you all right?" Jackie turned to Vera.

"Yes, I'm sorry. She came in this morning and has been sitting there all day. I didn't know if I should call the police or what. She wasn't disturbing anyone, and she didn't talk to any of the patients. Sondra said to just leave her and when it was time to lock up to tell her to leave. I didn't expect you back until Monday."

"Vera, it's all right. I expected she'd show up some day." Jackie smiled. "Just not this soon. I didn't see the newspaper this morning, so I had no idea."

"People have been talking about it all day," Vera said.

Joni bent down and picked up the paper and handed it to Jackie. She stood next to her as they read the article. "Wow, this cuts deep."

"No deeper than the hell she's placed you two through," Vera said between tight lips. Vera stopped. "By the way. It's good to see you both back here. I thought you were headed for Boston?"

Joni walked over and hugged her. "I came back here to talk with Jackie, and we bumped into each other at the airport." Joni blushed as she thought about the night they had spent.

Vera smiled. "Well, that's the best news I've had today." She hugged Joni again. "Welcome back, sweetie." She frowned at Jackie. "You are going to do right by her," she demanded.

Joni looked from Jackie to Vera. "Do right by me?"

Jackie shook her head and laughed. "Make an honest woman out of you. Vera's rather old fashioned."

Joni laughed. "Not to worry," she said to Vera. "We're going to do right by each other."

"Good." Vera slipped on her coat and picked up her bag. "Will I see you on Monday?" She asked Jackie.

"Yes."

"Good." Vera squeezed Jackie's hand. "I'm happy for you."

"Me too."

After Vera had left, Jackie took Joni in her arms. "I think we are alone. I'm sorry about this. I never expected Carin would be here."

Joni put her finger against Jackie's lips. "It's done. She's gone. I don't ever want to think about that woman again. I only want to think about this." She reached up and pulled Jackie to her. "I love you. I want to make love to you," she said softly.